Crave Saga
BOOK ONE

By

BERLIN DiVITTORE

ISBN
978-1-956529-10-4 (Paperback)
978-1-956529-09-8 (eBook)

This book is dedicated to my handsome husband and my number one fan! Thank you, John-Paul for always supporting my dreams and allowing me the opportunity to make them come true. You are my Sebastian!

Prologue

I ran down the hallway in the dead of night, as the blue moon shone in the window like a beacon, glistening against my bare chest and shoulders. My bare feet clapping the cold stone floor with every step. The faster I ran the further away she seemed to become but that didn't stop my legs from chasing her. Her bloody screams echoing the corridor.

"Briggita!" I shouted in panic.

"Sebastian!" she called back in pain.

Following the sound of her voice, I ran toward her bedchamber pivoting every turn and corner. I pushed against the heavy wooden door, but it didn't budge. It being the only thing that stood between me and the beckoning screams of my beautiful love. I took a step back and charged the door with all my might the door shot open. I stood in the doorway huffing and puffing as I scanned the room for my love.

She lay pinned to the ground at the foot of the bed, her clothes tattered, and her milky white breasts exposed. Her long brunette hair flailing about as she struggles to escape her attacker. The attacker took notice of me and continued to ravage my love against her will. He sat atop of her holding her hands with one hand, and with the other hand rustling with his pants exposing his cock.

He then began to dig through the layers of her dress. I stood paralyzed by what my eyes saw. Finally my instincts kicked in and I ran up behind him, locking his head with my arm and with one swift movement whipped him around and off her. His legs thrashing about like a tree branch in the wind, and his eye bulging out of his head as he ran out of breath.

My arm let go of the grip around his neck, sending his body flying, and finally falling to the ground with a thump. Once free of him, I quickly gathered my love from the ground. Still a bit rattled as she crossed her arms in front of her bare chest. I helped her to cover up with what was left of the fabric of her gown. I wrapped my arms around her and pulled her to her feet and then tucked her between myself and the wall.

Then turned back the attacker, expecting to see him lying on the ground but as I turned he was nowhere to found. Then my sister came charging through the door her night gown trailing behind her. Screaming, I reached out for her and I placed a tight grip on both her shoulders.

"Angelina, you need to calm down!" I shouted at her, while trying to make eye contact. Her eyes were stirring in her head searching her surroundings. I grabbed her face with both hands and pulled it toward mine looking her deep in the eyes and shouted.

"Angelina calm down!" Her eyes finally focusing in and filling with clarity. Once I was sure she was alright I grabbed her hand leading her toward Briggita, who had moved to the bed, I joined their hands.

"You ladies take care of each other. Do not leave this room! I will be back!" I kiss my beloved on the forehead. Then hastily ran out the door, following the echoes of screams and yells to the front of the castle. Finding a few of the servant huddled in terror.

"Where has he gone?" I bellowed to the cluster of maids that sat at the foot of the stairs. They said nothing for their mouth were still petrified with fear.

"Tell me!" I demanded, and then they pointed toward the entrance to the castle. Once more my feet moved quickly beneath me toward the front entrance, where he had left the front door open. It swung open and shut with the wind, clapping with every gust. I grabbed the large oak doors and flung them open stepping through the threshold. My keen eyes searching the darkness. Then

I heard a males' voice yelling from behind me. I turned, and there he was mounted upon a horse charging toward me.

"Sebastian!" He growled as he sped toward me, forcing me to dive out of the way into the dirt. Then rolling to my back, to watch him speed past me and down the path into the woods.

Then in the midst I began hearing a strange noise; beep, beep, beep it went. I stood and looked around for the source. I spun around looking but not quite sure what I was looking for. I had never heard a noise like that before.

Then I sprung upward, and my eyes shot open. I looked around in the pitch-black darkness of my surroundings. I saw nothing but the false red light emulating from my alarm clock, blinking on and off with every beep it made. I leaned over and switch it to off. I pulled myself to the edge of my bed, hunched over with my elbow resting on my knees with my hands on my face, rubbing my eyes.

No matter what I did I couldn't stop the memories from coming, at least for now they only haunted my dreams.

CHAPTER

I

My love life has always been pretty normal, nothing spectacular. That is until the love of my life, entered my life. I met him in the normal way: I hit him in the face with the door of a Porta-Potty at a concert. At least that is normal for me. But let's not get ahead of ourselves. If you're going to understand you need to hear the whole story.

I had just broken up with my year-long lover, Michael, who was not only my deepest and truest love but one of my best friends. I thought Michael loved me, I believed he did and I definitely loved him. Something I never thought I was capable of doing until we had fallen for each other. Yet somehow in the midst of all the feelings and passion, I never felt loved. Michaels version of love was great, but I guess it wasn't for me. All he ever wanted was sex, I mean, don't get me wrong. The sex was great and all, but I felt like there should be more to a relationship than physicality.

I can't believe I waited a whole year before I realized it would never change. Even though I was the one who left him I still felt a sting of loneliness. I mean we had been together almost every day for a year and suddenly he was gone.

So instead of letting me stay in for the weekend my girl Ashton convinced me to get glammed up and go to a concert with her. In hopes it would help me get over Michael, I mean there was a chance that it could happen. I figured I'd go because she said it would be her treat and I was heartbroken not stupid. No one in their right mind would say no to a free concert. Plus, there would be liquor if there is anything that helps a broken heart it's booze.

So, I did it, I managed to roll out of bed and cleanse my body of the weeks' worth of sadness I had been wading in. It's amazing how refreshed you feel when your whole body is covered in warm water. I stepped out of the shower and as I wrapped the towel around my body I began feeling revived.

Walking across the bathroom, from the shower to the sink, I paused as something caught my attention. It was my reflection, so I stood in front of the body mirror that hung on the wall and stared at the mirror image.

I gazed into my own eyes and thought; *will anybody ever be able to look at this face and say, "I love you"?* I mean I wasn't drop dead gorgeous, but I didn't look like a potato either. My face is a heart shape, with pretty high cheek bones, large pale green doe eyes, angel wing eyebrows, a small dainty nose and bow-shaped plump lips; that were usually coated in my signature boysenberry colored lip gloss. I have long wavy brunette hair, the shade of brunette most people mistake for black.

I am average height and curvy, what one would describe as pear shaped. As in I was lacking in the boob department, but I made up for it in the hips and ass department. Looking at myself in the mirror I took a step back and opened my towel, to observe what I really had to offer. I have cute feet and long legs, nice petite shoulders, and silky olive colored skin. I stood there examining myself naked in the mirror, turning and modeling different poses to watch the differences in my body with each pose.

"I would say confidently looking at yourself naked is a step in the right direction!"

I jumped and recovered my nudeness with my towel, turning to see who was watching me. Ashton stood grinning in the doorway, slightly giggling at my embarrassment.

"Oh my, I'm glad it's just you. How long have you been standing there?"

"Long enough to tell you are in serious need of a bikini wax."

"Ashton!" I said blushing and a little offended, covering my already covered lady part with my hand.

"Oh, don't act like I don't know what you have going on down there, I have a pussy too you know."

"Ew, Gross! Do you have to say that fowl word in my presence?"

"What? Pussy?"

"Yes,… that word."

"What is wrong with pussy?"

"What's not wrong with it, it sounds so…. well it sounds dirty," I said disgusted and irritated.

"Oh, is that all, you don't like it because it and I quote 'sounds dirty'" she said making air quotes with her fingers.

"Yes, that is all"

"Okay, just so we are clear I am not allowed to say the word pussy, pussy is the word I'm not allowed to say. Pussy, right?"

"Yuck!"

"Pussy, pussy, pussy" she began to tease. I covered my ears and ran from her like we were kids on the playground.

"Gross, stop it!" I screamed as I ran, hands over ears.

"Pussy, pussy, pussy!" The more she said it the more she saw it got to me and Ashton loves to poke at my buttons. And I let her because she is the sister I always wished I'd had growing up. That is what I envision when I see sisters. Two people who intentionally push the other's buttons because they love each other, and each of them trusts that that other person will be there always and would never deliberately hurt them. That is who Ashton is to me, I wish I had her when I was younger.

I'd met Ashton Livingston about seven years ago. I had just graduated high school and didn't see college being an option for me, all I knew was that I had to get away. I wanted to go somewhere amazing and exciting, I wanted city life. A life away from my crazy family and small town. I grew up in a small town called Rockland, Texas and the name couldn't have been more perfect if it tried. The town was pretty much rock bottom on the list of desirable places to live.

"It doesn't have much, but it has enough for the people who live here," is what my father always used to say. And it wasn't far from the truth, it had the basics like a Grocery store, Post office, Bank, and school system. That still wasn't enough for me, so I packed my suit case the day after graduation, bought a one-way ticket to San Francisco. I didn't have a plan, just the desire to be somewhere exciting.

I was sitting in a café a couple of blocks away from the Airport about to regret my decision to leave Texas. When I saw some chick walk in and start pinning up an orange flyer on the bulletin board by the entrance.

She seemed to be about the same height as me, with layered wavy brown hair, at about shoulder length. An oval shaped face and a small refined nose, and full lips but with a heavier bottom lip. She had a pretty rectangular frame, but her large perky breast did give her waist more of a cinched look.

She had a very hippie-chic sense of style, which completely clashed with my gypsy goth sense of style. She was wearing a long sleeve white lace dress, with a brown belt and brown scarf that hung down to her hips and brown suede boots. She also had a tan leather bag hanging from her shoulder filled with some books and a ton of flyers.

I don't know what it was about her in particularly that caught my eye, maybe it was the vibe I got when I saw her. I was someone who had no idea where I was going next and she seemed as if she knew exactly where she was going. I grabbed my things and headed toward the entrance where she stood. The closer I got the more I could see what the sign said:

'FEMALE ROOMMATE WANTED ASAP, RENT $500. CALL ASHTON AT (415)678-3190'

I saw that as a sign, pardon my pun, that I was meant to be here. From that day forward, she was always there for me, and became the sister I never had. It is because of days like that that I go out with her to random concert on nights like this. When I felt like all I wanted to do was hide under the blankets, eating pumpkin pie ice cream and watching sappy love stories like *The Vow*, *The Notebook* or even *Moulin Rouge*.

So, I got dressed in a sparkly spaghetti strap, put on my wedge boots. Throwing my long hair in a messy bun, did my makeup to hide the fact that I had been crying all week, and went out with my bestie for another Friday night concert. In hopes that she would work her magic and make me forget yet another guy, but this time it wasn't any guy, it was my first love.

Chapter

II

Ashton and I had been to many concerts together, it was kind of our guilty pleasure. Some girls go shopping, some dance on poles, some eat chocolate cake in the bathtub while listening to old Dolly Parton songs, we went to random concerts and danced like maniacs.

We made it to the concert in time and stood pretty much in the back of the crowd, right where we liked it. I know it sounds weird but it was easier to get out and there is not a whole lot of pushing and shoving but enough to make the experience real while remaining relatively enjoyable. We always seemed to head straight to the bar when we go to a concert and this night was no different. I don't know if it was the need for alcohol that lead us to the bar or because the bar was always the right by the entrance. All I know is I couldn't break a tradition. So, we downed a few drinks and had made it to the back of the crowd by the time the lead singer finished his intro.

We had no idea what the band was singing but we danced and drank and let go of everything. I didn't think about anything, except having a good night out with my best friend. By the fifth song, we were both ready to take our tops off and go home with a stranger.

"I told you this was what you needed!" She shouted over the sound of the loud speakers.

"Yes, I did!" I said before chugging the rest of my drink and throwing the plastic cup in the air.

"Woohoo!" we screamed as the remnants of the drink sprinkled on us like rain.

We continued to dance like we were crazy until the song ended. Then everyone began to cheer in unison for the band that I'm sure half the people here didn't even know. In the midst of all the cheering I felt Ashton tug on my shirt, so I turn to look at her. She motioned her hand for me to follow her and began pushing and shoving to get out of the crowd, so I followed her. Both of us shuffling through the horde of people until we were able to actually see the pavement again. We began to walk back toward the entrance and I hooked my arm in hers as we walked.

"Did you want to leave?" I asked a little surprised.

"No, I want another drink"

"Oh, that sounds more like you," I said with a laugh. She stopped walking and pushing me away as if she were offended by my comment. We looked at each other for a brief second and her glare of discontent changed to a smile. Then she reached out for me and laughed.

"Your right" she said, and we laughed together.

"Well you get the drinks, I gotta pee. I'll meet you at the bar."

"Kay" she said in agreeance as we parted ways.

It took me a while, but I finally found the group of porta-potties. They were in the far corner of the amphitheater, on the opposite side of the entrance. They were set up in two rows of three and the doors were all on the inside facing each other. So,

I held my breath and began walking between them until I found one that was empty.

I stepped inside and the air in there wasn't much cleaner and it defiantly didn't smell any better, but I had to go. So, if that meant going in a plastic building that house other peoples' feces and farts, I was going to do it. I took a deep breath and closed the door behind me.

After I finished my business I went to open the door, but it wouldn't budge. Turning the dial again to unlock the door. Thinking that I hadn't turned it enough the first time and gave the door another push, but it still didn't open. I was starting to panic as I was wrestling with the dial, turning it back and forth, but the door still wouldn't open. The more I tried it the more I began to panic. It was dark and smelled of other peoples' shit, I didn't want to die surrounded by other peoples' shit.

Just when I began to think I was running out of air, the door burst open and banged against something. Still holding on to the handle, and being the klutz that I am, I came tumbling out of the Porta-Potty right behind it. I immediately began to gasp for fresh air, breathing in deeply until I caught my breath. Then as I began closing the door I noticed a guy laying on the ground behind it. Then I remembered the thud I heard as I flew out of the poop hut. I closed the door and leaned over him, but I could barely see him due to the shadow from the wall of porta-potties.

"Um, hello. Are you okay?" I asked, as he began to stir grabbing his forehead with his hand.

"What happened?" he asked still a little out of breath.

"I think I might have hit you with my door, I mean the Porta-Potty! I mean are you gonna be okay?"

He began sitting up still holding his hand on his forehead, he sat there for a while, he was looking around as if he was lost. Then he tried to get to his feet, I tried helping him to stand the best I could.

"You sure you're okay to stand?" I asked.

"Yeah, it is just a bump on the head, nothing a little ice won't fix."

Then as he regained his balance he looked at me, and all the color seemed to be drawn from his face. He stared at me as if he was looking at a ghost, he didn't say a word or even move, he stared at me as if frozen in time.

"Is something the matter?" I asked unsure of what to do, "Um, hello you okay?" I repeated.

He began to shake his head back and forth like he was waking up from a bad dream. "I am so sorry for staring" he apologized grabbing my hands and kissing the back of each hand. "How incredibly rude of me."

Then still holding my hands he began to lead me out from between the group of small plastic outhouses. As we entered the orange light of the streetlights, I noticed he had a small bruise about the size of a quarter on his forehead above his brow bone.

"Oh, my goddess! Does that hurt?" I asked poking at the bruise as gently as I could manage.

"Ah!" He shouted as he grabbed my hand and pulled it away from his face. "So how about that ice?" he said with a chuckle, and a grin.

"Ok yeah, let's see about getting some of that for you." We walked toward the bar together.

"I'm Sebastian Baldovino," he said introducing himself.

"Jezebel Jones," I responded.

"It is lovely to make your acquittance Ms. Jones"

"I'm sure, too bad you had to suffer an injury at my expense," I said with a little bit of a giggle.

"Trust me, it's not as bad as it looks."

As we walked toward the bar I began looking Sebastian over, he was tall, I would say six feet even. He had quite a broad chest and shoulders, he had a pretty scrawny waist and arms. He made up for it however below the waist with thick muscular thighs and a nice perky butt, that his jeans seem to hug nicely.

He had a handsome face with a nice sharp jawline, and a protruding browbone that was covered by his thick but shapely brows. He had a tall refined nose, and luscious looking lips (for a guy that is) and he has very large dazzling amber eyes that are hooded by his brow bone. But the thing about Sebastian that is most unique looking is his hair, it is pitch black, thick and medium length, cut into a very boho kind of style. Meaning it was still quite long in the back, touching the nape of his neck, with flowing bangs that came down in front of his eyes every now and then. Kind of resembling Jonny Depp in a way, well if Jonny Depp was an anime character.

I could relate to his business punk style, he wore a gray v-neck under a white button up with a black leather jacket, deep blue skinny jeans and a pair of ratty old combat boots. That were not even laced up and open around his ankles. Beneath the collar of his shirt I could see that he was wearing a necklace of some sort but could not tell due to the fact he had it tucked under his shirt.

We finally made it to the bar and he signaled for the bar tender to come over, in the middle of making some else's drinks. The bar tender stopped what he was doing immediately and came straight over. Which was surprising to me, considering Ashton and I had just been here and it took us thirty minutes to get two shots. As the bar tender leaned over the bar to get Sebastian's order I began to study the bar tender.

He's about 5'11" and a bigger guy, not so much muscular just big. He was wearing black jeans, black biker boots and a black leather vest that was unbuttoned in the front. Showing off the nice rug of light brown hair trailing from his chest down his gut to the rim of his pants, and god only knew where it ended. Otherwise he was bald, he had a tribal tattoo on his right bicep, which I thought was odd because he was the whitest shade of white a guy could be.

Sebastian ordered a glass of ice and the bar tender got it for him right away, and then continued with the drinks he had previously been making.

I looked at Sebastian with my peripherals, as he held a glass filled with nothing but ice to his forehead. Then I felt a jolt deep inside my gut, no one had ever given me this feeling before. Who was this guy, I thought to myself, and was I making a mistake by introducing myself to him.

"How did you do that?" I asked trying not to sound to upfront.

"Do what?"

"Get the bartender to become your personal lap dog."

"Oh that," he said with a grin lowering the glass of ice from his forehead, "I own this amphitheater so that kind of makes me his boss."

"Oh of course you do. How silly of me." I said sarcastically, while smiling at him with amazement.

"So, what do you do?" he asked.

"Is this happening, your trying to engage in small talk, um okay. I'm a gossip columnist for Hourglass magazine."

"Oh, and what interested you in that line of work?" he prompted.

"I like people, but it is no secret that humans have a wild side, and that is my favorite part of them." The answer seemed to escape my mouth before I could even filter what I was going to say.

"What about you?"

"What about me?" I repeated slightly confused.

"Do you have a wild side?"

"I tried to live vicariously through others." I said trying to keep better control of my words.

"Oh, come on now we all deserve to be a little insane every now and then. Don't you think?" He said it as if he were trying to sell me something.

"I suppose, but I try not to get carried away." He did nothing but grin at me in response. We sat in silence for about three minutes, until I finally spoke up to kill the silence.

"Hey, so I gotta go find my friend but it was nice meeting you, and sorry again about your head." I began turning to climb of the bar stool. As I turned to step to the ground my attention was caught by something, or someone more like, standing at the end of the bar. It was Michael, he was standing there talking to some guys and laughing. What was I going to do now?

CHAPTER

III

I stood petrified, as if not moving would make him disappear or better yet make myself disappear. As I stared at him it was as if time seemed to melt away, and everything around me moved in slow motion. I watched Michael from across the bar laughing with his friends. It was then that I began to feel the hole in my chest start to swell. I began to wonder if he had ever loved me, all I was to him was sex. The swelling in my chest seemed to get bigger and stronger until it felt like it was going to burst. Still petrified and staring at him, then he turned, and we locked eyes. Then suddenly it seemed as if the stand still had all at once stopped and everything went back to normal. Then clenching my eyes shut trying to avoid any further eye contact, hoping it would magically make him go away.

"Jezz?" he blurted.

My eyes shot open, and as quickly as possible I turned away from him. Pretending as though I had not heard him, or I didn't know him.

"Hey, Jezebel." He said excitedly, then began to make his way toward me.

My cover was blown he defiantly saw me. I sat on the barstool trying to find a way to play this off. As I turned to looked up and saw him, my cover. I leaned in toward Sebastian, I spoke quickly but clearly.

"I'm so sorry, I know that I have caused you enough grief, but I really need a favor."

He raised his hand up, to calm me. "Hey, whatever it is I would be happy to help."

Then as he finished his sentence Michael had approached us, and without even thinking I grabbed Sebastian's face and slammed his lips into mine. My head was pounding and my heart what racing. Sebastian at first seemed very surprised and then he played along, and maybe a little to well as I felt him stick his tongue in my mouth, causing me to let out a little moan.

"Jezebel?" Michael said again.

I let go of Sebastian and turned to see who had said my name as if I didn't know it was Michael, I looked down at him from the bar. I began to play it off as if surprised to see him, ignoring the swelling lump in my throat.

"Michael! Oh, my goddess what are you doing here?" I said with the biggest smile I could manage.

"Oh, um Kyle, you remember Kyle, of course you remember Kyle, anyway Kyle got us some tickets to come see this band. His brother is working back stage and blah…" He spoke very quick doing a terrible job of hiding his nervousness, "What are you doing here?"

"Ummm I'm here, with umm," I said trying to think up a lie as quickly as possible. It was happening I was choking on the swelling lump, it was there in my throat I could feel it getting bigger. I grabbed my throat, my head still trying to think of something to say. Then as I was about to open my mouth, Sebastian spoke up. Stepping off the bar stool to the ground, he reached his hand out for a hand shake and introduced himself.

"Sebastian Baldovino, this is my theatre, you must be the exe." He spoke very confidently and with a smile, while vigorously shaking Michaels hand. Michael looked at him, then at me and then back to him, obviously star struck unsure of what to say.

"Michael Jahoba" he said in a middle of a nervous tone.

"Nice to finally meet you. I brought Jezebel here, so she could watch me work." Then leaned into Michael and in a whisper said just loud enough for me to hear. "Says it turns her on, naughty little thing, isn't she?" Then with a grin and a chuckle continued to shake Michaels hand.

"Oh, umm yeah naughty?" Michael responded intimidated, not just by Sebastian's physique but also his ego. Still holding Sebastian's hand and staring at him he said, "Hey it was real nice to see you Jezz, but I should get back."

Then all at once he broke eye contact and let go of Sebastian's hand, and began walk back from the direction he come. I jumped down from the barstool, Sebastian turned to face me giving me a sideways grin and leaned in.

"Thanks for, umm well that, I should be going this time." I said as I began slowing backing away, "It was nice meeting you and great concert Kudos, kudos, umm well bye." Then turning I hurried away before I could embarrass myself any more. Just when I thought I was finally out of view I turned back around to look at him again and he was gone. I scanned the entire bar, but he vanished and all I saw were to empty barstool where we once sat. I tried not to make anything of it though, so turning away and began searching for Ashton.

Walking back to the entrance there was no trace of her, so I took out my phone to give her a call. I scrolled through my favorites list in my contacts and clicked on Ashton. Then to my left I saw something light up in the darkness of the ticket booth. Still holding the phone to my ear, I began walking toward the booth. With every step I took I could hear some familiar music which also emerged from the ticket booth. Then as I peered in through the little window I quickly regretted it. I saw Ashton shirtless and groping the ticket guy, playing an aggressive game of tonsil hockey. I looked away and closed my eyes trying very hard not to blow chunks. Hanging up the phone, I tucked it away in my back pocket. Then I approached the booth again and knocked on the door.

"Hey Ashton, sweetie, I know you having loads of fun but we gotta go."

"Is it time to go already, I just started having fun." She said with her mouth full of someone else's tongue. Then I heard him start moaning heavily, and movement from inside the booth.

I opened the door and regretted it even more than the last time. Ashton hand her hand placed firmly around the shaft of his penis. Which emerged fully erect from between the open flaps of his unzipped denim jeans. She stroked him as she ferociously kissed his mouth.

"Okay, yup your drunk." I said as I reached inside the booth to pull her out, "Come on time to go home." She rose to her feet the best she could still gripping the ticket guys cock. "Ashton, honey you gotta let go of his penis."

"I didn't let go yet?" she said confused.

"No, you didn't let go yet," I responded.

"Oh, oops!" then she burst with laughter, then she let go and he grabbed her hand.

"Come on, you don't have to go yet" he said clearly talking through me as if I didn't exist.

"Yes, she does." I retorted grabbing her satchel and her shirt from the booth floor. Throwing Ashton's arm over my shoulder, we began walking out of the amphitheater. The ticket guy stood in the doorway of his booth his cheeks, mouth and neck smudged with pink lip stick, and his dick still hanging out of his pants.

"What the hell am I supposed to do about this?" he shouted disappointed, gesturing to his erection.

"Not my problem," I shouted carrying Ashton out into the parking lot. Rummaging through my bag and pulled out the keys, unlocked the car and plopped Ashton into the passenger seat and then I us drove home.

As I drove I began rolling over all the events of the night in my head. Well that night was a bust, I thought to myself. Then I turned to look at Ashton passed out, using her seatbelt as a pillow, at least it wasn't all bad.

However, I did meet someone, even though he will probably have a bruise for a couple days. He was good looking and that kiss, I would consider seeing him again. I still couldn't let go of the fact that Sebastian had disappeared like that though. It didn't make any sense, and the way he looked at me. Who was Sebastian Baldovino, and should I reconsider?

Chapter

IV

The next morning, I woke up took a shower and made breakfast. Sitting at the kitchen counter drinking a steaming cup of earl grey black tea and scrolling through my social media. Which included lots of pictures of my sister and her kids, my Mom's food pictures, and some pictures that I had posted of Ashton and I getting ready for the concert. There were also pictures of Michael and his friends getting trashed last night at the concert. Then as I was scrolling I came a crossed a photo that Ashton had posted of her and ticket guy. I started at the picture for a while, and then continued to scroll.

Then as I took a sip of my tea, Ashton came tumbling into the kitchen. Wearing only a magenta colored bra, some fuzzy shorts with rainbow zebra stripped, and long teal knee-high socks. That flopped off the end of her foot, with one sock scrunching up around her ankle.

"Good morning," I said cheerfully.

"How did you sleep?"

"Like an unconscious unicorn who was shot in the face with a moose tranq," She muttered picking at the plate I had filled with crispy turkey bacon. "Where is the coffee?" she growled

"I didn't make any, but you are welcome to have some tea."

"Yuck, I will not put that filthy leaf water into my body. It will probably feed my inner child and I've worked too hard to shut that bitch up. I need something bitter and loaded with caffeine." Even though Ashton dressed like a hippie, her personality resembled more of a biker chick. That was something that made her special and I loved that about her. In all honest she actually loathed all things organic and mother nature worthy.

"Sorry, you will have to make some." I said still scrolling.

"Well you're feeling better I see."

"Well gossips not gonna write itself."

"That's the spirit, there is some pathetic soul out there waiting to be tormented by the harsh words of Jezebel Jones. The people cannot survive without gossip and it is because of those people you have a job, you should be very grateful." She said filling the coffee pot with water, and then pouring it into the coffee maker.

"Thank you! Oh, wise one, you always know what to say." I responded sarcastically making a bowing gesture with my free hand and head, before sipping my tea.

"Okay, sister you better watch yourself before I sick Mojo on you." Mojo is our nine and a half pound, black and white pomksy. We both turned to Mojo, who had been sitting on the couch in the living room across from the kitchen, he sat upright at the sound of his name. He let out a very cute little bark and started wagging his tail excitedly. Then we looked back at each other and laughed.

"So, did you even get his name?" I probed, with a bit of a maniacal grin.

"Did I get whose name?" she asked clearing trying to shuffle through her hangover to remember the details of the night. Then

I held up the picture she had posted, and her face went completely pale at the site of him. She slowly placed her coffee mug softly down with one hand and grabbing the phone from me with the other. Staring wide eyed and pale at the picture, she remained still.

"What the fuck is that!" She finally blurted, as if snapping back to reality.

"That would be the ticket guy, from the concert last night. I gotta say Ash not the best one. I think the librarian guy from three years what cuter than this guy. At least he had all his teeth." I teased her, as she continued to look at the picture.

"I think you might be right." She responded with a scrunch up nose and half-closed eyes, as if squinting her face would make the picture disappear. "Ugh! Take it away! I can't look at it anymore." Then sliding the phone across the counter top back to me.

"Well I mean, hey he…" I began trying to find something positive about him, to make her feel better, but then coming to a halt as I realized there was nothing I could say to make it better. "Yeah, I got nothing this one is really bad."

"I know!" She shrieked in embarrassment. "Ok, go ahead tell me. How bad was it? Are we talking like first base, or like second? Third?" Then she paused and held her breath in preparation for what came next. "Oh, sweet gherkin, don't tell me we hit home base?"

"Remain calm you were like mid-run between second and third. Your virtue is intact. Just not my eyes, I will never be able to unsee that. I also hope you washed your hands because you have ticket guys special parts all over them." Then she looked at her hands as if scoping them out for coodie-germs with the naked eye.

"Ew! Gross!" Then turned around to the kitchen sink behind her and began to scrub them clean. Then after about five whole minutes of Ashton boiling and sanitizing her hands, she finally turned around with a look of relief on her face, as if she washed away not just the germs but the entire experience down the drain.

"So, we all know how my night ended. How about yours?"

"How about my what?" I asked clarifying her question.

"Did anything strange or exciting happen to last night or was it normal."

"Well first off nothing is ever normal when you are around. Secondly, I had tons of fun last night and I met this interesting guy, oh and I ran into Michael. Then I had to practically pry your hands of some guys..."

"Ahhh, hey, hey ok we get it, I need boundaries! Let's move on now." Ashton said cutting me off, "Lets back up a little, you saw Michael? Last night? At the concert?" I didn't say anything, I just nodded in response. "Oh, honey I'm sorry the whole point was to get your mind off him."

"Yeah, but it wasn't too bad, I mean he looked happy, and seeing him like that did kind of help. I mean, yeah, I wasted a whole year on loving him, but I guess I can know for sure now that all I was to him was a booty call. That's me Michael Jahoba's booty call." As I finished the sentence my eyes began to swell up with tears. I tried my hardest to force them down but there was no helping it. My heart was broken and when your heart is broken it over powers you head every time. So, I broke down in a full-on sob fest.

"Oh, come here sweetie!" Ashton said in her best mom voice, coming toward me with open arms wrapping me up in a hug. I started crying into her chest, as she held me while stroking my hair. Then when I was finally done crying I unburied my face and lay on her perky pillows.

Then she pulled away from me, cupping my face in her hands to ensure direct eye contact, she said in a sincere voice. "Hey, you said you met someone last night right, that's gotta be a good sign. Let's talk about that instead."

Which I must admit is my favorite thing about Ashton, and probably the number one reason she is more than my roommate, she is my heart sister. The fact that she can be a

Badass-Psycho-Super-Slut, but she can also be an Optimistic-Genuine-Caring-Soul, who is always capable of finding a silver lining.

"Yes, okay." I answered through snot and sniffles, reaching for the napkin holder that always sat on the kitchen counter, and wiping my cheeks dry.

"Was he cute? Did you get his number?" Then I nodded, paused, and then shook my head as I blew my nose into a napkin.

"Well which one is which honey, I'm getting mixed signals here. Was he cute?" I nodded.

"Did you get his number?" I shook my head.

"Well did you get anything from him?"

"Yeah, his name is Sebastian and he actually was the owner of the Amphitheatre where the concert was held." I didn't even realize it as I spoke until I was finish. I was starting to feel warm inside my chest and my stomach started to flutter and I began to blush. Then my mind drifted back to our kiss, even though it was rushed and unintentional it was still very enjoyable. His soft plush lips and his warm tongue and the way he held me.

"Oh, you like him!" Ashton teased.

"No! I don't!" I said, defending myself and suddenly snapping out of the warming sensation I was in.

"Yeah, okay." Ashton responded in a deepened sarcastic voice totally not convinced. "So how did you meet this Sebastian guy? I mean he sounds like big stuff. How did *you* possibly run into him?"

"Oh, I umm, well I sort of…"

"Come on spit it out!" She prompted.

"I smashed his face with the door of my porta potty." I said as if ripping of a metaphoric band aid of my embarrassment. As I finished the sentence Ashton erupted with laughter. Then as her laughter began to break and she began to catch her breathe.

"And he still talked to you after that?"

"Yes, I helped him up then I walked him to the bar and we chatted a little and that is when I ran into Michael." I debated telling her about the kiss, but I wasn't even sure if it was that important of a detail.

"Well I'm glad you had a good night, now we can move on instead of you moping about the house all day. I mean, I understand, you need to cope but you've had your time and now it's time to move on. And hey for all you know this guy could be the key to that."

"Speaking of moving on, I'm gonna go. Before you start making me kiss your ring and feed you grapes." I said sarcastically.

"Where are you going?"

"TO WORK!" I shouted with artificial enthusiasm, walking out of the kitchen throwing my fist in the air.

Entering the room that I liked to call my studio, because even the word office gave me anxiety. Studio made it sound more creative and fun. I sat at my desk looking at my email to see who my resent gossip was to be about, opening a blank word document. I stared at the blank page for about five minutes, and then I began to write.

Chapter

V

My one true love, my love for the written word. I have always loved writing, ever since I was a little girl I loved to write. But I don't think it was the writing that I loved. It was the stories and the foundation of what it meant to write. I fell in love with the idea of imagining things and recording them on paper. As if writing them down not only made them permanent but true.

I was lying on the sofa in my studio with writer's block. Thinking about what angle and what amount of grace to approach my new outrage with. Just because I'm a gossip columnist doesn't mean I have to be a bitch. I think that was what our readers, and my editor and chief Miranda Gills, liked so much about my gossip. Whenever I had writers block, I liked to lie down and think about why I do what I do in the first place. I close my eyes get all snug and think back to when I was young, discovering books for the first time.

I'm not gonna lie I am a bit of a fantasy fanatic, but my older brother Charlie used to call me a Fairytale Whore. I love all things fantasy and magic, *The Hobbit, Harry Potter*, and even *The Chronicles of Narnia*. If it had strange creatures, magic, and a bit of romance, I was there front of the line with my strawberry jam jar. I'd filled with all the money from every birthday card, every holiday, every A on my report card and all the tooth-fairy had given me. But as I got older, I had to think of more inventive ways to earn the money to buy new books. The lemonade stand was too mainstream for my taste, so I sold muffins.

I mean get real who doesn't love a delicious, moist, soft muffin and it also catered to my second love my love for baking. So, I would walk around town and ask people if they wanted a box of freshly baked homemade muffins. As soon as I had enough I would walk down to the city library (the only good part of the town I grew up in), tell Ms. Wanda, the librarian, to order me a book and give her the jar full of cash. Then of course being the honest person that I am would go home and bake a lot of muffins and deliver them. Which I didn't mind because it gave me something to do until my book arrived.

As a young girl I had always dreamed that one day I would have a story to share with the world. I would write about dragons, and magic and some amazing tale with this amazing hero. Yet, here I sit day after day in front of my laptop, writing about another celebrity scandal or politicians affair. I mean don't get me wrong I love having a job, but it's too 'real life. The whole reason that my love for fantasy blossomed was because real life was too plain for me. I loved the idea of living in a world where unusual things happen every day. Except in that world it's not considered unusual it normal and exciting.

I do often get into a position in my job where I sit back and think 'I am gonna do it, I am gonna quit today and I am gonna write for myself again.' But then reality hits and I remember I am a grown ass woman with bills to pay and a puppy to feed. So, I continue the path of self-suffocation and put off my dreams to make ends meet. I have been writing for Hourglass magazine ever since I got to San Francisco. Actually I was a waitress for about six months first, then one day I was reading the local wanted ads and I saw an ad for a news reporter. So, I sent in my résumé and some writing samples and got a call two days later for an interview. I have been named employee of the month going on three months now. Not to brag or anything. It's not brag worthy material anyway seems clear something about this job agrees with me.

However, it also seems clear that something about me doesn't quite agree with it. I couldn't figure out what it meant, it pays good and it has great benefits. I only have to go to the actual office three days out of seven, we only print once a month and I am employee of the month; for which I get a bonus and you'd think an extra $250 in my pocket would be enough to shut me up. It's my job and somebody has got to do it, so I suppose why not let that somebody be me.

Like I had told Sebastian last night, I like that people have a wild side, I wasn't lying when I said that. I actually did enjoy living vicariously through all these crazy people and reporting on all their crazy schemes. I am not ashamed to admit it either, I am the tattle tale of the media and that is the best part about my job. I know that sounds sick and twisted, but something about catching people in the act of doing something scandalous feeds to some crazy ego that I have. It makes me feel powerful and not like a little kid steal cookies kind of power. More like a I'll blackmail you for everything you own kind of power.

That very well may be the reason that every time that some crazy notion pops in my head to quit and follow my heart to share my stories. This crazy power demon wakes up and slaughters that notion, and I find myself back at the office.

So, I lock myself away in my studio and contemplate all this while I write about something that someone did that they shouldn't have been doing. This month it was "The Donna" or rather Donatella Carmella Dandridge she was some big stuff in the tabloids lately. She was mostly famous for cleaning her house in lingerie on a "hidden" camera on a site that she had created for herself called 'Donna Does It Again'.

Aside from being completely shameless and bold on camera she is also an heiress and the wife to famous golfer Giuseppe Maserati. However, this month I think she would rather be the wife to the catty guy and least that what her lips seem to think. That is where I come in, but I am having trouble after taking all last week off and having from my heart broken didn't help much either. Something about heartbreak seems to mess with people and change them. Then there was a knocking on the door.

"Hey sweetie, it's Ashton I brought you some dinner." She said muffled from the other side of the door.

Dinner? Did she say dinner, we just had breakfast! I opened my eyes and sat up on the couch to look at the clock and was shocked because it read 7:36pm. Had I been in here all goddamn day and not gotten anything written, boy was I losing my touch. I rush to the door and cracked it open.

"Hey Ash!" I said in a yawn.

"Hey! Your supposed to be working in here, not napping." She said a little irritated pushing the door open and flipping on the lights. Then morphing into her mother-phase she began storming past me to the desk setting the plate of food down.

"I haven't been sleeping." I nagged.

"Oh, yeah! Then show me what you been working on?" Then I rushed around the desk and slammed my laptop closed. That was open to the half-blank word document that I have been working on.

"That's what I thought!" she began growling at me and began storming back out of the room.

"I have been working!" I said defending myself. As if I were in high school all over again and I was trying to explain the big fat C on my report card to my parents.

"Then why can't you show me the proof."

12"Why the hell do you need proof. Shouldn't you trust me? Why the hell you are nagging me for in the first place." Seeming to have stumped her with that one. Practically seeing the train of thought inside her head come to a screeching halt. Then she sighed and walked back toward me.

She said in a soft voice as if embarrassed someone might here her "Jezebel sweetie, I am worried about you. I don't know what actually happened between you and that jerk Michael, but he got you honey. He got to you good, I want you to be happy. I just miss the old Jezebel. I have hated seeing you all depressed for the past week or so. Sorry if I got a little carried away just now."

"A little?" I teased, making her face turn bright pink. "I completely understand, and your right he did get to me and now I can't so much as keep track of the time, little lone write."

"I'm sorry, well maybe you should wait one more day."

"No, I can't, we can't afford to wait one more day."

"Hey, now don't you worry about that we're sisters aren't we? I can cover your half of the rent while you get your life back on track and your heart sown together."

"Thanks." I said with a smile, then I looked down and saw the plate that she had brought into the room. "Uh, Ashton sweetie what is that?"

"Chicken stir fry with mushrooms and broccoli."

"Isn't broccoli supposed to be green?" Then took my finger and poked at something I suspected was supposed to be broccoli, "This is gray."

"Hey! I made that for you out of the kindness of my heart."

"By that you mean that you bought a frozen meal cooked it in the oven and dumped it on a plate. Now you are trying to claim it as your own."

"Yup, pretty much," she confessed. I loved Ashton, but the girl couldn't cook a grilled cheese on a tin roof in July.

"So how about we go downtown and get us some real Chinese stir fry?"

"Sounds good! Last one out the door is paying." She said racing for the door.

"Hey! I thought we recognized my financial struggle!" I shouted as I chased after her.

We both wrestled with our shoes and jackets and then were out the door and into the car.

CHAPTER

VI

Jumping out of the car and rushed inside the restaurant out of the brisk night air. Then we took our seats at a table and the waiter handed us a menu and told us he would bring us some tea. I began scanning through the menu, then looking up at Ashton, who was not scanning her menu but staring at me.

"What?" I asked a little frightened by the grin she was giving me.

"Oh, nothing waiting for you to decide on what you want to get?" Then I flashed her a look raising my eyebrows, giving her the 'you can't be serious' look.

"That's really why your staring at me?" I asked the question aloud, but she didn't say anything just batted her eyes at me a little. Then I probed her, "Well, what are you getting?"

"The Beef and Broccoli stir fry of course." She replied with more than the appropriate about of sassy, raising my eyebrows again. "What you said, 'let's go get real Chinese stir fry' so here we are getting real Chinese stir fry."

"So then why are you staring at me? Why can't you be a normal friend and pretend to go to the bathroom, instead of interrogating me with your eyes?"

"Fine." She said get up from her seat if I am not back in time order for me, you know what I want. Oh, and get me a cocktail too, I don't care what it is as long as it has alcohol." She let out a little giggle at her own joke, then walked away.

I went back to studying the menu, and not two minutes later our waiter returned with our tea. Placing it on the table and took out his notepad, took our order and rushing back off to the kitchen. I began looking around at the other people in the restaurant. There were a lot of family's, and some younger high school kids and a couple on what was obviously a date. But that's was not what caught my attention.

I was drawn to a booth far off to my right of this elderly couple. I watched as the man, with his shaking hand grabbed a napkin. Then he slowly, but steadily began wiping sweet and sour sauce off his wife's chin. Then smiled as I saw her chuckle, because she didn't even know it was there. Then she looked at him adoringly, clearly thankful to have this man to take care of her. Then I felt my stomach tighten and looked away as a cold tear rolled down my cheek, I wiped it with my hand.

Ashton was right Michael did get to me, he was my best friend and my first true love. That was supposed to be us, 50 or even 60 years from now. The part that hurts me the most is that the entire time we were together, knowing somewhere inside of me that my image of being with him forever was never going to be real. I was fooling myself. At the same time, I didn't want to leave him because I loved him so deeply and it didn't matter if it was a lie. Yet here I sit here alone in a Chinese restaurant waiting for someone to sweep me off my feet for real and love me for my soul, not my body.

"The bathrooms here are so cold. I felt a draft in my cooch as I was peeing. Don't you just hate that?" Ashton said, coming back to the table.

"Yeah, it's the worst," I said choking down the feelings I had just evoked about Michael. Then our food came and as I was unwrapping my silverware out of my napkin, I glance back over at the elderly couple. They were getting up to leave and he was helping her out of the booth. Then with her jacket and purse, they made their way toward the door. "It's the absolute worst." I muttered under my breathe.

"What was that, hon?" Ashton said with a mouth full of noodles.

"Nothing!" I said drawing my attention away from them once more, and rejoining Ashton at the table. "Let's eat. Doesn't this look good?" Then dug my fork into a big pile of lo mein noodles.

We stuffed our face full of Chinese took down a couple cocktails and a good two hours later we were headed out the door. I was tussling with my jacket, as we were walking toward the door. My arm was searched for the arm hole in my jacket, I looked back at the table to make sure we didn't leave anything, having a district feeling that I was forgetting something. Then as I turned back around, arms flying through the air, I was brought to a sudden stop. Because I had just punched some guy in the nose, as my hand finally freed itself from the tunnel of my sleeve.

The man grabbed his face and turned away from me, bent over and groaning.

"Oh, my goddess! I am so sorry! Are you okay? Is it bleeding?" I began to panic.

"No, I will be fine, but you have one hell of a swing on you." He said as he began to straighten up and then turning to look at me. I couldn't believe my eyes, was this really happening to me? I wanted to die, and everyone in the restaurant knew it too. They were all staring and were all witness to my face turning bright red.

"We have to stop meeting like this." He said in a cool husky voice, still holding his hand to his nose.

"Uh, yeah, you sure you're okay?" I surveyed, finally getting a look at his nose after he finally removed his hand.

"Oh yeah nothing a little ice won't fix." Then flashed a sparkling smile at me with a wink. I blushed but this time from the butterflies not the embarrassment.

"What's going on?" Ashton said joining in, slightly out of breath from running back inside.

Then snapping out of the luring hypnosis that his smile gave me, and I floated back down to earth. "Ah, yes, Ashton Livingston I'd like you to meet Sebastian Ba…" then paused as I tried to remember his last name.

"Baldovino." He chimed in reaching his hand out to Ashton, and she took it.

"Oh, Sebastian Baldovino. Well its very nice to me you. Jezebel has told me all about you." She said through a smile and wide eyes.

"Oh, well my forehead has taken worse hits than a plastic door. I do have to say however my lips did enjoy the second hit she through at me." He said jokingly and with a small snicker. Both Ashton and I stared at him wide eyed and were both silent for a while. Then trying to break the awkward silence he had created he continued by saying. "She is a wild one this friend of yours."

"I'm not quite sure I know what you're talking about?" Ashton say confused and way out of the loop. Not sure what to say next Sebastian stared at her then at me, then back to her and finally at me. His lips moved but no sound came out, as if he was trying to find the words to say, but the words weren't finding him. Then I finally broke the silence before he had the chance to explain what event he was referring to.

"Well it was nice see you again, sorry about, uh well, your face but we should be getting home now." Then I began pushing Aston toward the door.

"Oh, now wait a minute," he began but then I cut him off before he could say anything else.

"No, we really should be going now." Then escaped out the door and began walking down the street.

"What the hell was he talking about?" Ashton inquired.

"Oh nothing. It was a joke." Then let out the most convincing fake laugh I could manage. Ashton not convinced stopped walking, folding her arms, cocked her hip and started to scowl at me.

"Ok fine I'll tell you. The night we met at the concert, after I walked him to the bar and got him some ice, I…I mean we, well we, I might of… kissed him." I said the last words in a hush voice hoping that if I said it quite enough she would let it go.

"You did what?" she snapped.

"I kissed him, okay!" I shouted my response. She didn't say anything her mouth just dropped open. Then I rolled my eyes at her and began walking away. Then she let out a squeal and ran to catch up with me.

"Are you for real?"

"Yes, look it's not that big a deal okay." I said trying to hide my smile.

"Bitch, if it's 'not that big of a deal' then why didn't you tell me before?"

"Because, I didn't mean to kiss him."

"What does that mean?" Ashton asked completely confused.

"I didn't mean to kiss him, I panicked, Michael was walking toward me after I had just been staring at him from across the bar. I didn't want it to seem like I was a pathetic broken mess, or even make it known that I was gawking. So, I panicked and asked Sebastian to help me."

"So, what you kissed him and then pretended like Michael wasn't even there." Ashton joked as we walked along the sidewalk.

"Well."

"You slut!" she retorted back hitting my arm.

"Ow!" I blurted rubbing my arm and blushing. "So, you're not mad I didn't tell you?"

"No, I mean maybe a little offended that you thought you had to keep it a secret. I mean who are you talking to, you had to pry my hand off some guys willy." Then we giggled a little. Then she continued, "So, how was it?"

"Soft, warm and a lot of tongue."

"Gross! I was talking about Michaels reaction. Well talk lip locking details later, I am not mentally prepared for it yet."

"Oh well he was, it was well he…" Then I was cut off by the sound of my name being called followed but the sound of approaching footsteps. We both stopped and turned to see who it was, Sebastian was running after us, and looking at each other intrigued.

"Jezebel!" He shouted, even after I had turned to look at him.

"What!" I shouted back.

"You left this at the restaurant." He replied out of breath as he handed me my cell phone. Then a I looked at it I reached my hand deep into my coat pocket to be sure that's where it was. Then realizing that he was right, took the phone from him and put it in my pocket.

"Thank you." I said in a shocked but very grateful.

"You came all this way to return her cell phone." Ashton countered, obviously challenging Sebastian's motive.

"I guess I figured she would need it." He countered back, making direct eye contact with Ashton. The two of them then began dueling in a staring contest like it would determine the alfa.

"That was very thoughtful of you." I said breaking through the indiscernible ice wall that was building between them.

"It was my pleasure." Sebastian said breaking eye contact.

"Ha I win!" Ashton blurted but we both ignored her childish response.

"How else was I going to get your number?"

"Smooth," Ashton teased. Then once again raising my eye brows at her, she backed off, and she began looking at the display window of the clothing store we had stopped in front of.

"Yeah, I suppose you have a point. I mean I'm sure your insurance company may need my contact info if your nose ends up being broken." Then we both chuckled into the night air, our breath floating separately and then becoming a single cloud that blew away in the breeze. He stared at me with the same dreamy eyes from the first time we met, and a grin that seem plastered on his face. Then smiling I said, "Do you have a piece of paper? Or a pen or something?"

"Uh yes. Here," then he took out his smart phone and keyed in his code and opened up a new contact screen and handed it to me. I typed in my name 'Jezebel Jones' and my number '(415)678-2494' then hit Save.

"There you go!" I said handing the phone back to him and smiling.

"Thanks!" he began, "so I guess I'll call you sometime."

"Yeah, it would be nice to run into you on purpose, and not make you bleed or bruise"

"Yeah." Then he looked away, with a smile as if amused by something other than the inside joke that I had made.

"So, I hope to hear from you soon!" I said interrupting his daze.

"Me too." He said with that same grin.

"Well, see yeah!"

"Goodbye," he said grabbing my hand and kissing it, making me blush. Then he turned and started walking back toward the restaurant. Then I turned away slowly, not having taken my eyes of him yet, smiling.

"Okay we get it you're a fuzzy pink schoolgirl with butterflies, can we go home now? It is starting to get cold." Ashton complained at me, jerking me toward the car.

"Yeah, let's go home."

Then we continued to walk down the street toward the car. As we were walking Ashton had started telling me something about having to go back to work tomorrow. I was only half listening because all I could think about were Sebastian's eyes and the way that they didn't look through me but into me. Like he was staring directly at my soul and tickling it with his smile. Then through the flutters of butterflies I was feeling in my stomach I felt something buzz.

I took out my phone and opened the text it read; *'Ms. Jones I would be honored if you would please join me 'on purpose' this Friday night at 8pm sharp for a lovely dinner-SB'*

And I wrote back *'I would be glad to join you, p.s. I'll bring the ice.'* I got a response almost as quickly as I had pressed send. *"I will have my driver pick you at your apartment building. Please wear something formal-SB.'*

Then wrote back, *'I can't wait!',* waiting for the response but nothing came. So I tucked my phone away in my pocket and felt a warm sensation in my chest as if the hole was getting a little smaller. Then I smiled approaching the car, arm and arm with my heart sister who was still yammering on about going back to work tomorrow. Then I remembered I had to go into the office and still hadn't gotten any work done. I began to mentally prepare myself for what lie ahead.

CHAPTER

VII

"Where am I?" I called out into the darkness, my voice echoing without end. Everything was blurry, and it was quiet. I began running to see if I could find someone to help me. I was barefoot, wearing a white dress, that fluttered behind me as I ran, and my feet clapping against the ground. It was dark and foggy, and as I ran I saw an orange light in the distance. I began to chase it, then as I got closer it multiplied. Then it multiplied again more and more lights seemed to appear the closer I got. They were lined in two rows, one to my left and the other row to my right. Then I my feet stopped, as if they knew where I was before I did.

I looked around the fog making it hard to see anything except shapes and shadows. I began walking to figure out where I was, if I know where I am then I can get out. I crept through the darkness my feet shivered with every step against that cold stone floor. Then

I figured out where I was and was overwhelmed with fear. I turned to run the other directed. As I turned a creature with large blood red eyes lunged at me, I screamed.

My eyes shot open and I sat up in bed, feeling my surroundings. When I was able to place myself in my bed, relieved all my body parts were in order. I sighed turned to look at the clock, it read in bright green lights 1:48am. I sighed again and through myself back down onto my pillow. Still shaken up about the nightmare that had happened. I combed my fingered through my long hair against my roots, coming to terms with the situation. I didn't even understand what it even was, nothing in the natural world like that ever happens.

I could barely remember anything about the dream, it was as if my mind had blocked it off already. All I knew was it didn't feel real, but I told myself that it was a rabid dog. In hopes that it would help me get over the incident and be able to move on with the rest of my night. That what I should do, so I turned back to the clock on the night stand and it read 1:55 am.

Then I closed my eyes and tried to go back to sleep when I hear my phone buzzing on the night stand next to me. I opened my eyes to see my bedroom illuminating with the light from my phone, I rolled over on my side to grabbed it. Squinting I tried to read what was on the screen, but the light was to bright and blinding. Throwing off the blankets and turning on the lamp on my night stand. Patiently waited for my eyes to adjust and looked down at my phone. It was a text from Sebastian.

'I am so excited to see you, I cannot stop thinking about you -SB.' This made me smile and I suddenly forget all about my nightmare.

I replied, *'I just saw you.'* I began thinking back on all the times I'd seen Sebastian, as I sat waiting for a responds.

Starting from the time we'd met, and he seemed like the last person in the entire world to ever be interested in me. I mean every time we saw each other something went wrong. One of us ended up bleeding or injured and usually that someone was him. After all the times that I'd hurt him he still wanted to go out. Then my phone vibrated in my hand I blushed as I read his response.

'I know, and I have already been away from you for far too long -SB.' I sat with warm cheeks enjoying the butterflies in my stomach I never thought I would feel again. I didn't even know what to say back, lucky I didn't have to because my phone chimed again. I looked down at my phone, *'I know we scheduled our date for this Friday, but I don't know if I can wait that long. What are you doing tomorrow? -SB'*

'Tomorrow is Monday so I have to work tomorrow, but I am free the day after. Do you think you can wait one more day?'

'That sounds perfect, until next meet Ms. Jones -SB'

'Goodnight, Sebastian.'

I sat waiting for him to say goodnight back, but nothing ever came. So, I put my phone back on my bedside table and turned out the lamp and crawled back under the blankets. I closed my eyes in hopes of dreaming a better dream with the heartwarming thoughts of Sabastian.

Chapter

VIII

I walked into the office in a daze, I was the epitome of the walking dead. It had been so long since I had been to the office, I forgot how loud and bright it was. But I drug my feet against the gray carpet, to my cubical. I threw my coat on the back of my chair and my purse in the filing cabinet, plopped down into my chair. Then began to start up my computer, I stared as the loading wheel spun around and around on the screen. Then snapping out of my trance as the login screen popped up. I entered my username and password and then had to wait again for the computer to unlock.

As I waited I noticed my desk had become very dusty in my absence. So, I pulled out the giant cylinder of Lysol wipes I keep in my filing cabinet I had begun wiping down my desk. I had done just surface of the desk before I needed another wipe. I pulled another wipe out of the container. Then from behind me I heard someone yell my name, quite loudly might I add.

"Jones!" Completely startled I jumped, dropping the open Lysol wipes contain on my desk. Spilling cleaning liquid all over my desk and it began to drip on the carpet just beneath my desk. I turned with a pinched scowl to see who was calling me and I was prepared to give whoever it was an earful.

"What do you want..." I began snarling, "Miranda!" I said with a smile, changing my mood like a I was a chameleon taking on a new color, she grinned back at me. "What can I do for you?"

"You can explain to me why you have been sick for so long, you called in so many times I was starting to get worried. Yet here you are fit as a fiddle." She said leaning in to my personal bubble, and then leaned back.

"Yeah, I'm sorry I had to take a couple mental health days."

"Oh, well as long as we are feeling better and it is not reflected on your work." She said the words very slowly, as if she were talking to a kindergartener.

"Yes, I am fine now, I just need a little time to adjust back to the way things used to be." I said through my teeth, holding back what I'd like to say. "Thanks for..."

As I began the sentence her phone rang, and she put her hand up to my face, and pulled her phone out of her pocket.

"Hello!" She said with I wide smile plastered onto her face, then I heard an inaudible voice on the other end of the phone call. A voice to which Miranda replied "Ravi! Yes, baby! Talk to me about the photos." As she listened to what the man was saying on the other end of the phone, she pointed to me and then to my chair. Which obviously meant, that we were finished talking now and to get to work. So, I sat in my chair and spun around to my desk as Miranda began walking away. Leaning back in my chair into the aisle, I turned to look at her as she strutted between the cubicles toward her office, in her peach color knock off brand pumps. Miranda Gills was and interesting woman, she was absolutely gorgeous on the outside. But on the inside, she was something else, something rotten and poisonous.

She was probably about 5'11", I say probably because she always wore heels and I wasn't quite sure how tall she actually is. She has golden blonde hair, cut inches from her scalp, with long bangs. Deep blue, almond shaped eyes and full plump lips that were always caked in a fresh layer of Barbie pink liquid lip stick. As far as body type goes she was straight up and down. At least that what I assumed by the pant suits she always wore a few sizes too big. I actually find her to be quite beautiful, the essence of a Barbie. That is why Ashton and I always referred to her as Office Barbie.

Well we do it partly because of her looks, but also because of her personality I will describe it in one word, Plastic. As in synthetic, she plasters a fake smile on her face and walks around like Miss high and mighty. Just because she is management, as if that makes her better than the rest of us. She is what my mom would say is "good in theory not so good in practice." As in a great worker who gets stuff done, is respected and successful. But in any form of a person face-to-face confrontation she is a rude-snobby-bitch made of plastic.

I do fortunately end up only having a one on one moment with her a few 5-8 times a month, and even less if I'm lucky. I respect her as my boss but as a person I'd like to take that smart phone and shove it where the sun doesn't shine.

I brushed the conversation Miranda and I had just had off my shoulder. I began cleaning up the Lysol liquid that was spilled all over the desk and floor. Then as soon as that was out of the way I got to work doing some research for my article on Donna. I found the normal cyber stocker information like birthday, height, even more personal stuff like family history. Then as I began digging deeper I found out that Donna was going to be in town for an event. She was going to be staring in an actual movie, that they are going to be filming right here in town. So, opening my email I began making arrangements to get on the set to interview her. I also made arrangements with one of our photographers to come with me. Another one of my favorite parts of my jobs is that I get to be like a crazy stalker paparazzi, and honestly clam to be working.

I went about the rest of my work day with ease, writing interview questions and getting a solid outline made up for my article. Then before I knew it was time to clock out, I was gathering up my things and was on my way out the door when it happened again.

"Jones!" This time it didn't startle me as much, but I did stop dead in my track. Then pivoted on my feet in a one eighty turn. It was Miranda again, and she was looking at me like I was forgetting something. I didn't know what to say, but what I did say still wasn't the best choice.

"What now?" I regretted saying as soon as I heard myself say it.

"Excuse me?" She piped up and raising her eyebrows at me. Scanning the room and I could see that everyone was watching us.

"Miranda, I'm sorry I don't know where that came from. I was …" she put her hand up to my face again, I immediately stopped talking.

Then she turned and pointed in the direction of her office. I began walking with my head down like I was a dog who peed on the rug, except this rug was my boss. I walked into her office Miranda entering after me closing the door behind her and proceeding to her desk. I was standing in the same spot like a dummy, it was like my head and my feet were no longer on speaking terms. I began to feel so uncomfortable, my head was telling me to stay, but my feet were telling me to run for the hills. I looked at her sitting at her desk gesturing, quite calmly, for me to have a seat. Which made me feel a little better, so walking toward the desk I made myself comfortable. Then I looked at her and smiled, which was mistake number two.

"Wipe that smirk off your face!" She growled at me. I did so immediately, curling my lips inside my mouth. "What is the meaning of this attitude, it is not very professional, and I will not have it. You may be a good writer Ms. Thang, but you're not that good!"

"Yes, Ma'am." I meant the words to mean I understand, but they came out as sarcastic. My brain began to panic, why was my body rebelling and not doing as it was told.

"Is that more sass Jones?"

"No, Ma'am." I took a deep breath finally something that came out the way it was supposed to."

"Now that is more like it. Now listen here Jones this office space is a hive, I am the queen and you are my worker bees. You know what happens to a worker bee when it has finally serviced its queen?" I know that she said it as a question, but I could not allow my mouth to make another mistake. So, I said nothing just looked at her, patiently waiting for her to answer. Rolling her eyes at me and answering her own question. "They die! Your talented baby, but one more slip up and this queen bee might just decide your time is up. Am I making myself clear?" I nodded.

"I said, AM I MAKING MYSLEF CLEAR?" She snapped at me like I had eaten the last piece of cake at her birthday party.

"Yes Ma'am!" answering back clear and precise, trying hard to hide the fear in my voice.

"Good, glad we had this little chat. I hope you have a nice night." She said plastering her smile back on her face.

"Thanks, Miranda what was it that you need?"

"Oh, you're right. I saw that you are going to be Triple O tomorrow," in work speak that means Out of Office. "Go ahead but I'm going to take your camera guy, you can take a picture with your phone or something."

To keep myself from hitting strike three for the day I just said, "Will do."

"Okay, now get out." With those words I gathered my things and was out of her office and into the elevator faster than you could blink. I was standing in the elevator when my phone started vibrating. Checking my phone, I noticed that Ashton had called me three times, so I called her back.

"It's about time." She said answering the phone.

"I am sorry I was in with Miranda. What's up?"

"In with Miranda? That sounds hot, I was wondering how you were gonna get her to be okay you missing so many days!"

"Does everything have to be an innuendo with you?" She didn't say anything she just laughed. Then the elevator stopped, and the doors were opening, and I continued stepping out of the elevator.

"So, I have a surprise for you? Where are you at?"

"I'm walking through the lobby, I will be home asap."

"No just come outside! HURRY!" She barked and then hung up the phone. Completely confused I put my phone in my pocket and walk out to the side walk. I began looking around and becoming more and more confused.

"Hey, Jezebel!" I heard Ashton shout from my far left. I began walking toward her all rushed. I finally reached her, and she continued.

"Look at what I got!" she said as she presented her brand new sparkly metallic lime green convertible like one of those girls on a game show.

"What is that!" I said excitingly, completely pushing the work day behind me.

"That, my friends is my brand-new car!"

"How could you afford this, and why didn't you tell me you were gonna get a car."

"I have been saving up, and I wanted it to be a surprise. After the way life has been treating you lately I figure you could use a good surprise to cheer you up!"

"Thanks Ash, for surprising me with a car that you bought yourself." I sarcastically said with sisterly sass.

"Don't mention it," she said completely unharmed by my sass, "So, you want to cruise?"

"Hells yeah I do!" both jumping in the car and pulling off from the curb and we speed down the street. Away from the hive and the horrid reality of worker bee society.

Chapter

IX

The wind blew through my hair as we drove around in Ashtons new convertible. Looking around at the city around me as it all became one big blur of lights and buildings.

"Hey, how was your first day back to work, since the falling out?" Ashton said interrupting my daze.

"It was okay. I had a bit of attitude slip with Office Barbie."

"Oh, tell me?" Ashton said the words like a starving cat who only survived on the gossip of my work life.

"It wasn't anything to crazy. I was heading out the door and she wanted to ask me for my cameraman? She called out my name and I may have made it a little too obvious that I didn't want to be there."

"So, did you get in trouble?"

"No, she gave me a reminder that I am 'replaceable.' Like I didn't already know that."

"Like anyone would want to work in that nasty hornets' nest. You can still quit you know."

"Ash, we have been through this. We can't afford to live off the one income."

"Honey, I told you it is okay if you want to quit. We will make it through. We still have some open positions at the theater -that I know you would be perfect for." Ashton said with that optimistic voice that she always has when coaching me through my life.

"Yeah, I'll think about it. Hey, can we change the subject now? I had kind of a long day. How was your Monday back to work?" I said as we drove downtown toward our apartment building.

"I'm sorry to hear that you had a bad day honey, I wish I could do more. My day was the same as it always is, working on the choreography for the show. Today we did costumes after lunch and tomorrow we are going to do our first full run through." Aston said the words full of excitement, like she always did whenever she got a chance to talk about her work. Ashton is the choreographer and director for the Midtown Theatre.

Right now, they are in preparation of their annual Halloween play. This year they are doing something written by someone local; an exciting fantasy thriller called Night Terrors. I am not quite sure I know what it is about, and Ashton doesn't like to give out spoilers. I can respect that, neither do I, but it would still be nice to know before she forces me to go. This way I could mentally prepare myself before I had to pretend to be interested. On the other hand, Halloween is my favorite holiday, and she has yet to disappoint.

"I'm so excited to see the show. I am so glad that you find so much joy in what you do."

"I mean it is work but sometimes we do have a little too much fun. Listen to me honey, I know what you really want to do is write. But you used to tell me that what you really loved to do was be on stage, maybe this is a sign."

"I said I would think about it Ash, beside I enjoy going to watch just as much."

"Okay, but so you know we still are still casting for the Fairy roll and I am hoping we find someone soon. I mean it is quite challenging to do my job if every roll isn't cast and we have already made it to dress rehearsals." I rolled my eyes as she rambles on about her job. "I mean we have had some girls try out, but I don't get the vibe I want from these girls. It sucks that our original fairy fell off a horse but that's showbiz."

Then as she finished her sentence, we pulled into the parking garage underneath our apartment building. I had never been in the parking garage even once since I moved in with here. To be completely honest I forget we even had one. Ashton pulled into the lot labelled RM 512.1.

"I had no idea we had our own personal space down here." I said.

"Yeah, every room does, its included in the rent." She responded.

"Why does it have a point one on the end of the number?"

"Oh, because our apartment is a two bedroom it comes with two spaces. That one is yours." She said as she pointed to the empty spot behind me, as I step out of the car. "You mean you haven't been parking in the garage the entire time we have lived here?"

"No, I guess I was okay with where I park. Which reminds me, you're gonna have to take me to work tomorrow. I left my car there because of your little surprise here." I said gesturing to her new convertible.

"Isn't it great! I always wanted a convertible." She said it with the biggest smile on her face.

Then we began walking through the parking garage talking about what we should do for dinner. When out of the corner of my eye I saw a shadow behind the row of parked cars to our left. I discreetly looked to find out who or what was casting it. I couldn't see anything; it didn't help that the lighting in the parking garage sucked.

So, I turned back to the conversation. Then once again I noticed something, or someone move from behind one vehicle to the next to my left. This time without any discretion I turned quickly to catch a glimpse. Once again, I saw nothing.

"What do you keep looking at?" Ashton exclaimed, clearly a little annoyed.

"Okay, I don't want to spook you but there is something over there behind those cars. I think it is a person watching us." I whispered as I inconspicuously pointed to the shadows along the outer wall.

"What do you mean watching us?" She said as she began to scan the shadows looking for someone.

"Hey, don't make it so obvious that your looking." I said from between my teeth with a fake smile and pulling on her.

"There is nothing over there anyway, let's get inside it is freezing." My gut was telling me that I knew I saw something, but the rest of me trusted Ashton. If she said she didn't see anything then I will believe her.

We were halfway across the parking garage almost to the elevator. When I saw something again, and this time I know that I for sure saw someone. There was another person with us in the parking garage, and they were defiantly following us.

"I saw it again!" I said interrupting Ashton talking about some guy she hired as her new makeup director. I said the words still looking forward, once again being as discreet as possible.

"Wha...what?" she responded so caught up in her story that she barely caught what I said.

"I saw it again; I know for sure that I saw someone!"

"I don't know what you're talking about sweetie. I don't see anything." I was starting to feel a little paranoid and a tad bit angry that I could see it and she couldn't. So once again I blew it off and we continued walking we were almost to the elevator anyway.

Then the car alarm on the vehicle to the left of us suddenly went off. We both stopped dead in our tracks, letting out a quick squeal and held on to each other as the car continued to sound. We stood frozen realizing that it was just a car alarm. Probably set off by a pigeon or something, we straightened out. We both began to catch our breath to slow our pounding hearts. The two of us were still standing in front of the car, when she quietly asked me a question.

"Was that you?" I said nothing just stood petrified with fear. "Honey, are you okay? I still didn't say anything and there was a moment of silence. Then I spoke with my eyes bulging, barely moving my mouth, "Ash…" I began to whisper, feeling her lean in to hear me better. "Do you see it now?" I asked still hardly moving.

She followed my line of sight to find out what I was gawking at. Then she let out a weak gasp, and then took a deep breath as if she was about to scream. And I knew she finally saw what I was looking at. From out of the darkness was a set of glowing, blood red eyes and a shiny set of fangs peeking out from behind one of the cars. I grabbed her hand, "Ash don't scream."

We both stood shaking and quivering with fear, not believing our own eyes. Then I heard her whisper into my ear, "Are those…?"

"Eyes," I said finishing her sentence for her. Then it was as if she was reading my mind. We both instantaneously began walking slow backward toward the elevator.

When suddenly the car moved, and not in the normal way that cars move. It was as if something exceptionally large was moving between them pushing them apart. We both screamed and took off running toward the elevator, screaming the entire way there. I swear I heard a noise that resembled a growl as we ran. Then the row of cars to the left of us seem to each be shoved backward. Like something was moving fast between them and the outer wall of the garage causing them to jolt toward us.

Running as fast as we could, finally making it to the elevator doors. Ashton pushed the button to summon the elevator, I could hear it coming down the shaft. Ashton was pushing the button frantically, as if it would make the elevator come faster.

I looked around the garage I didn't see anything the thing seemed to disappear. Then I heard the elevator ding, turning around to get in but noticing the door hadn't opened yet. So, I began tapping on the doors with my hands, continuing to squeal, Ashton joining in right beside me. Then the doors parted open and we both jumped inside and press the 5 button and the doors closed slowly. Then as the elevator began ascending upward, I stopped screaming and finally began to catch my breath.

Neither of us said a thing, or even looked at each other as the elevator continue to move. Then we reached our floor and stepped out of the elevator and began walking down the hall. Ashton took out her keys and started unlocking the door. We both threw our self's down on the couch, sat in silence for a couple minutes, then turned to look at each other.

"What the hell just happened?" we said in complete unison.

"I have to say for my first time being in the parking garage, I didn't like it." I said still slightly out of breath.

"Things like that don't happen!" Ashton said sounding confused. She said the words as a question. I didn't think she was asking me, but I answered anyway.

"Well, you never know…" I began trying to be as optimistic as possible and giving in to my writers' way of thinking. Then was interrupted by Ashton as she stood up and began yelling frantically.

"NO!" she began, "Things like this **DO NOT** happen in the real world! It makes absolutely no goddamn sense! Nothing in the physical world, humans or animals, could not have big-giant-bloody-red-glowing eyes like that. Okay?" She paused and when I was about to open my mouth to say something she started up again. "It had fangs too. Not regular canines like the normal teeth of a person, or even an animal. That thing had blades where its teeth should be, fangs! Covered in slime and drool and god only knows what else. It didn't even have a body! How could something with giant eyes and knives for teeth, have no freaking body?"

Then she froze, she didn't so much as blink, and her eyes started to bug out of her face. I stood up and placed my hands on her shoulders. "Sweeties are you gonna be okay?" I waited for a while for her to answer but got no answer. I sat her back down on the couch next to me, still stiff.

I sat there reflecting on the events of the night. I realized that I had seen that creature before, last night in my dream. Come to think of it almost resembled everything about what happened. I had somehow predicted it. I didn't even know if it could be considered a prediction. This is so surreal, I did not know how to react to such an event, let alone a dream that happened the night before of the exact event. Then I began wondering how it was possible to be able to have dreamt of an event before it happens.

Then I got up and helped a still shaken Ashton, to bed. I tucked her in; then I went into the kitchen and made some chamomile tea for the both of us to calm down. I poured two mugs and mixed them with some honey, I brought Aston's to her room and left the mug on her bedside table. I grabbed my tea and headed into my room, I took a couple sips and sat the mug down.

Sitting on the edge of my bed staring blankly into the void, in disbelief and shock. Then out of nowhere my purse began to sing. I jumped up and dug through my purse and pulled out my phone. It was my Mom.

"Hey Mama." I said in a nonchalant tone, as convincing as I could manage.

"Oh, Sweetie, I am so glad you answered!" she said excitingly.

"You are? Why?"

"I wanted to know if it would be okay if I come to see you soon?"

"Oh, that would be…uh amazing." I said the word with as much enthusiasm as I could manage.

"Honey are you okay? You sound little strange?"

I held the phone to my face and thought of the words my mom had asked me. I wondered if I should tell her, or would she think I was crazy. As I thought I felt my eyes glaze over I continued to stare into space reflecting until the world became one big blur. I began to compare and contrast the creature from dream to the one we had seen downstairs in the parking garage. My mind began to drift until my eyes no longer worked and all I could see was the images in my head coming to life.

"Jezebel? Darlin' answer me!" my mother shouted through the phone that I was still holding to my face. I jumped as her voice traveled through my ear cannel, until it made its way to the processor in my brain. I made my way back from my trip to la-la land and I remembered that I was on the phone.

"Ahhh," I shouted "Uh Mama, I'm sorry I can't talk right now. Sorry I gotta go." Then I hung up the phone and threw my head back and took a deep breathe. Then a couple minutes later my phone rang, and I answered it immediately.

"Hey Mama, I am sorry I hung up like that. It is not a good time right now…" then a man's voice broke through my monologue and cut me off.

"Jezebel?" The voice said, and I was suddenly confused.

"Ummm, yeah?" I responded unsure of what else to say. Then there was a brief silence as I began to reroute my train of thought. "Who is this?"

"It's Sebastian. Is everything alright?"

"Yeah, I am fine. Sorry I just got off the phone with my mom and I am in a bit of a weird headspace right now."

"I understand. Are you alright?"

"I will be fine thanks; I'll call her back later. Did you need something?"

"I just wanted to check up on you?"

"Like I said I will be alright. Wait why would you need to check up on me?"

"Uh, I am generally concerned for your wellbeing is all. Actually, to be honest I did have another reason for calling. I wanted to make a slight adjustment to our date this Friday. Would it be alright to get together tomorrow night when you get off work instead?" he asked sounding a little worried.

"Okay? Could I ask why?" I said trying to avoid anymore more confusion and distress on my brain.

"I would like to see you sooner than planned. That's alright, isn't it?"

"Yes of course it is. Tomorrow night is perfect, I can't wait to see you."

"Yes! I will have my driver, Jasper, pick you at 6 o'clock sharp. I will send you a picture of him so that you will know how to recognize him but trust me he isn't hard to miss."

"Okay…" I blushed and giggled a little like I was a small girl again talking to my crush on the playground. "Goodnight Sebastian."

"Goodnight, Ms. Jones." I began holding my stomach with my hand as he said the words. Feeling as if the butterflies were going to come bursting out. I heard the line disconnect and I hung up the call and lay back on my bed. I closed my eyes and pictured his face and his gorgeous amber eyes and dazzling smile.

I was literally almost eaten alive by some invisible thing that shouldn't even exist but all I could think about right now was Sebastian. Crazy how he always made the bad feelings go away. I didn't feel bad anymore, not even my own mothers voice had that kind of a calming effect on me. With my eyes still closed I thought back to the kiss that Sebastian and I shared at the concert. How good it felt to kiss him. I thought back so hard, it was almost as if his lips were still pressed against mine. Then I drifted off into a deep sleep to the warm thoughts of Sebastian Baldovino once again. What was this mysterious felling that hung on him like a cloak? And was it a good or bad kind of mystery? I can't wait to find out.

Chapter

X

I was standing in the bathroom brushing my teeth thinking about the romantic rendezvous I had with Sebastian last night in my dream. I as my toothbrush stoked my teeth, I giggle at the butterflies that were tickling my stomach. I rinsed my mouth, and as I bent down to spit out the toothpaste infested saliva. I froze at a strange sound, bent above the sink I realized it was someone screaming. Listening a little closer and then tracing it, it was coming from Ashton's bedroom. I quickly spit and ran across the loft to her room.

I threw the door open; she was in bed wrestling with her comforter screaming like someone was hurting her. Her arms and legs flailing every which way, from beneath the blankets. I approached the bed and tried to get a hold of her and dig her out from underneath the bedspreads.

"Ashton, sweetie, I need you to calm down!" I shouted trying to get control of her motions.

"No! No! No!" she said screaming as she began pushing away from me with her whole body. She pushed against the bed sliding all the way to the other side.

"Ash no don't..." before I could finish, she flew off the bed and landed on the floor with a giant thud. Still standing next to the bed trying my best to look over the top of her now empty queen-sized bed, to the pile of blankets that she was engulfed in on the floor. She had stop moving and screaming for that matter.

"You okay honey?" I asked reluctantly, to which her only reply was a groaning sound. Then I made my way around the bed, grabbing the blanket and began pulling until she came tumbling out. I through the now empty comforter back on the bed and looked at her still crumpled up on the floor. She slowly lifted her head to look at me, and through squinted eyes she simply asked, "So, do you want some breakfast?"

"I could eat." I respond as casually as possible. Then we both smiled at each other in amusement, I reached my hand out helping her to her feet.

I was scrabbling the eggs, when Ashton finally entered the kitchen and began pouring a giant mug of coffee.

"So... you want to talk about your fight with the bedspread this morning?"

"Um, no...not really. I am just a little shaken up about last night is all. I had a nightmare, but I mean how could I not. But it is all over now so let's just move past it, like I said it probably wasn't even real so not too big of a deal." Then she walked around the bar and took a seat on one of the barstools. I passed her plate of eggs, sausage, and toast in front of her on the counter. She picked up her fork and stared at the plate. Reading all of the obvious signs of shock on her face, her eyes bugging and her facial expression not existent.

"You sure it's not a big deal?" I asked trying my hardest not to cause her anymore trauma.

"Yeah, I want to move on and pretend like it didn't happen, because it is impossible." She said the word firmly, as if trying to convince even herself. Ashton was an overly optimistic being, but she was also a realist. Even though she saw the creature with her own eyes, as I had, she was clearly in denial. "Let's move on and get things back to normal. Change the subject." She demanded finally starting to pick at the food on the plate in front of her.

"Ok well, my mom called me yesterday."

"Oh, what did she say?" she responded excitedly, obviously forcing the mundane conversation.

"To ask if she could come visit soon."

"Okay, I love your mother. She cooks really good food."

"Oh, good because you get her all to yourself, I'm not in the mood yet to speak to my mother."

"So, what are you just gonna avoid your mother?"

"Yes, I am and besides, I have a prior engagement and I don't want to cancel."

"Why is seeing your mom such a bad thing? I know it hurts honey, but you need closure and hiding your breakup is probably not the best way to get it." she said clearly feeling loads better.

"Your right it's not and I love my mama, but I just want to bury it and move on and that is not possible with my mother around. She liked him so much she was already talking about grandkids and he hadn't even made a proposal yet. I don't want to have to explain to my mother that I got her hopes up wasting a year of my life with a man who isn't going to be the father of her grandchild. I am finally starting to feel like I am free of him. You know, I am moving on finding closure, and all without my mother."

"Oh. I know what, or should I say who, this is really about," then she paused and there was a moment of silence "Sebastian!"

she blurted with a grin. I blushed at the sound of his name and I tried not to grin back but was unsuccessful.

"Wow! You guys made a connection fast. Well, I am happy for you but just know I want you to be careful going into a new relationship so quickly."

"Thanks Ash, I know it is risky. And not to be corny or anything but a part me felt connected to him from the moment we met. I know that sounds crazy, but I feel something different when I am around him, or even just thinking about him. It is a feeling like I have never felt before."

"Well, you are right that sounds a little bonkers, but I am not going to question your heart. Again, I only ask you be careful whose hands you entrust it to."

"Yes, oh wise one," I mocked sarcastically. After a brief silence I looked at her and said, "I hope my mom could be as understanding about it as you are."

"You know your eventually gonna have to tell her about Michael. Besides, she is your mother she just wants you to be happy. You could always sugar coat it by telling her you have found a new guy."

"I barely know him; we haven't even been out together yet. I know I said he gives me a great feeling which he does, but there is also something very odd about him that I can't place. There are somethings that have happened since I met him that still kind of give me chills."

"No, not the chills." She said sarcastically teasing me.

"Stop it! I'm serious. Like when we first met, he stared at me really creepy like. Or him disappearing into a crowd of people within seconds. And he called me last night after, well you know, like he knew that something had happened. He said it was because he was just checking in, but what a coincidence. That is just so happens to be when we are both almost killed. How can that be possible?"

"Those are honestly the worst excuses to be paranoid I have ever heard. I am not going to let you just stand him up. Go on one date with him first and get to know him. You are psyching yourself out. I totes understand you just got out of what you believed to be a profoundly serious relationship. And feel like that guy betrayed you but not all men are gonna betray you the way that scum bag did. Okay?"

"Ok, one date…which by the way is tonight."

"Well good luck, but first work. I am gonna hop in the shower quickly and then we will head out." Then she started to walk away, stopped in her tracks, turned back, and grabbed her coffee mug off the counter then continued her march to the bathroom.

CHAPTER

XI

I was walking out of the office after a long day of chasing down Donatella Camellia Dandridge. Heading toward my car confidently having had finished my article at work and looking forward to my date with Sebastian. I drove home planning out my outfit in my head. I pulled into the recently discovered parking garage making my way to our section. Combing the lot as I drove and making sure there would be no surprises this time. I walked toward the elevator trying hard not to make any noise. My stomach felt a little tight and I could feel the goosebumps on my arms getting bigger with every step. I was three quarters of the way there when one of the orange lights to my left began to flicker. But this time I was not staying behind to investigate. So, I took off toward the elevator at the best run I could manage in my high heels.

I walked through the front door feeling the paranoia wash away as I passed through the threshold. Entering the apartment to find Ashton sitting on the couch watching audition tapes and making notes. I began walking toward my bedroom.

"Someone had a special delivery." She said the words in a high voice as if mocking me.

"What are you talking about?" I asked confused, looking around the loft for some sort of a package. "Did you order something?" I asked still very confused.

"Not for me, but you did." she said playfully, "It's in your room." Then she gestured to my bedroom with a nod. I turned and walked toward my bedroom a little hesitant, unsure of what was going on.

Opening the door to my bedroom the door creaked, and I couldn't believe what I was looking at. Laying on my bed was a navy-blue gown, and next to it sat a box of what I assumed would be shoes to match. I approached the bed and caressed the gown with my fingertips and almost melted at the touch of the gown. It was velvet material so soft and so luscious, still petting the material of the dress I looked at the box.

On top was a single red rose and there was a small note tied to the rose. I read the card and blushed, it read: *'I thought you would look beautiful in this -SB.'* I brought the flower to my nose to smell its sweet fragrance. I smiled as its silky petals tickled my lips and nose. I closed my eyes and imagined the petals to be his lips. I stood there inhaling the scent and fully embracing the butterflies.

"Fancy dress." Ashton said plain from the doorway, as if she was unimpressed. Then she began to make her way toward me. "Where are you going?"

"I, uh… I don't know." Still a little stunned by her surprise entrance.

"Oh! You were right he is mysterious, and so romantic." She said as she grabbed the flower from my hand and read the note. I began opening the box to reveal a pair of sparkly black pumps with an ankle band.

"What time is he going to be picking you up?"

"He said he would send his driver at six."

"It is 5:32 now."

"What!" Then I turned to check the alarm clock that sat on my nightstand. I looked at it as the last number changed from a two to a three. "I have to get ready!"

I grabbed the dress off the bed and ran into the bathroom. Fifteen minutes later I stepped into the living room wearing my new outfit. I had touched up my makeup a bit and tossed my hair up into an elegant but messy bun, with accents of hair around my face.

"How do I look?" I asked Ashtons who had gone back to watching her audition tapes.

"Like a princess!" She said with a big smile on her face.

"Thanks, I am so nervous. Then I checked the time on my phone 5:57. I have to get going. Jasper will be here any minute now."

"Have fun!" she shouted from the sofa as I closed the door behind me.

I made my way through the lobby and out the front door of the building. There in front of me was a black Mercedes SUV and who I assumed was Jasper. He was stand with holding the door to the back seat open wide.

"Ms. Jones," he said the words in a monotone sounding voice, but he said them with a smile. I climbed into the back seat and anxiously waited to see where Jasper would be taking me. The door closed behind me and drove away from my apartment building to the unknown. I took a deep breath to steady my nervous heart.

CHAPTER

XII

It was quite and adventurous drive, but we finally made it, as the car began pulling up to the entrance. I was momentarily taken from the real world at the stunning sight of what I saw just beyond the glass. The entrance to the grounds has a giant black gate, hinged to two beige colored brick columns standing erect on both sides. The gate was already propped open in anticipation for our arrival. The columns were connected to the beautiful brick wall that seemed to stretch for ages, surrounding the perimeter of the mysterious fortress. There were trees and hedges beautifully placed across the landscape.

We drove up a long gravel road and toward a roundabout that sat in front of a breathtaking mansion. In the center of the roundabout was a small fountain, with flowers decorating the outside edges of the roundabout. The car stopped in front of the footpath to the front doors. Jasper opened the car door and offered me a hand. I stepped out of the car and was escorted toward the most beautiful place I had ever seen.

Walking up the pathway, between the small hedges and lights that were perfectly placed on both side of the path. At the end of the walkway was a flight of wide stone steps. We climbed the steps, and made our way through a large set of wooden French doors, beautifully carved with rose patterns. The doors closing behind us with a soft thud.

"Just a moment madam I will fetch the master." Jasper said before disappearing through a doorway off to the left.

"Master?" I mouthed the words, not sure if the guy I had met at the concert was the same man.

Waiting inside the largest vestibule I had ever laid eyes upon. I continued looking around, becoming more and more amazed with every new visual experience. The stone walls are covered with paintings of all sorts, and some antique weaponry. The entire room has stone floors and are blanketed by a beautiful red carpet over the entire perimeter, and that continued to trail the huge "A" frame flight of stairs in front of me. The top of the stairs breaks off in two separate directions with a beautiful stone banister. But the thing I couldn't take my eyes off of is the beautiful chandelier dangling from the high ceiling. I gazed at the beautiful light that it gave off, shimmering and sparkling like a crystal web.

"Beautiful, isn't she?" Turning startled by the voice, I saw Sabastian standing behind me with a gorgeous grin on his face, his amber eyes twinkling at me. Dressed in a nice black suit, with a gray collared button up, this look brought together with a burgundy tie.

"Oh yes, she is amazing." I said taking one last quick look at the chandelier, and then facing Sebastian again. He let out a small chuckle, then leaning in and he said, "I wasn't talking about the chandelier."

"Oh," my face flashed red with embarrassment and flattery all at once. "Well then thank you. This gown is gorgeous, and so is this place."

"You like it I wasn't sure when I picked it. I was afraid it would not compliment your natural beauty but now seeing you in it I feel confident in my decision." I responded by smiling brightly at the compliment but remaining silent. Moving on, Sebastian continued, "I wasn't sure if bringing you here would be appropriate for our first date, I didn't want to overwhelm you. However, I am so confident in what I feel for you, and I am hoping the feeling is mutual."

"Do you live here?" I asked the question with more force than I had intended.

"Yes?" Sebastian responded to the question unsure if it was not the answer she wanted to hear.

"That is amazing, I would have never figured you for the fancy type."

"Fancy type? Well, I suppose that is a compliment."

"Oh dear! I am so sorry how rude of me…" I said covering my mouth but then he cut me off.

"No, no it is alright, I am only teasing you." Then he let out a small laugh, smiled and put out his hand, "I hope you are hungry."

"Yes, I suppose I am hungry." Placing my hand in his and he began escorting me into one of the huge archways that sat perpendicular to the stairs. We walked down a long corridor lined with small lanterns that lite the way, as well as some décor, picturesque statues, paintings, and antiques. We passed several closed doors before we made it to a set of elegant French doors. He opened the door and then stepped aside, holding the door for me. Then ushering me to my seat at the beautiful elongated oak table that stood in the middle of the room.

We sat and talked for what seemed like a long time but was realistically only about forty-five minutes. Then Jasper approached us with a cart and placed our plates in front of us and poured us each a glass of red wine. We sat eating the best meal I had ever had, starting with a gourmet salad with French dressing. Followed by a stunningly cooked steak with some red potatoes and French cut green beans on the side. Then for dessert we had a chocolate crème cake with strawberry glaze and whipped topping.

We talked and laughed the entire time, enjoying each other's company more and more with every word. We talked about every topic you could think of, connecting on every level. Then before I knew it two courses and a long conversation later, four hours had gone by in what seem like no time at all.

"Would you like to see my favorite part of the house?" He asked me with an eager smile planted firmly between his ears. Nodding in excitement, we got up from the table and left the dining room. We walked back through the corridor in the direction from which we had come. Reentered the great hall and slip back behind the stairs. Down another long corridor, that was equally as exquisite as the last, and into a courtyard behind the house.

The courtyard blanketed in hedges trimmed at about hip level. Together they formed a breathtaking labyrinth. The way was lit by torches scattered about the courtyard. Standing still holding Sebastian's hand in astonishment and speechless. Before I could say anything, Sebastian took off racing through the labyrinth.

"Hey wait for me!" I shouted trailing after him. I followed him the best I could in the soft glow of the torches, and my four-inch heels.

Chasing him all the way to the other side of the maze. When I finally caught up to him, he was standing inside of a quaint little white gazebo surrounded by rose bushes. I looked up at him holding his hand outward for me to grab it. Taking his hand and walking up the few steps into the gazebo then turning to face the direction we had come. The gazebo sat opposite the manor, so we stood and gazed at the posterior end of the house. It was a magnificent sight with its beautiful architecture and huge windows. We could see the servants inside the manor moving about and lights turning on and off.

"It's so amazing that you get to live here." I said softly breaking through the silence of the night air. "I guess I can understand why this is your favorite part of the house."

"Oh, this isn't my favorite part, this is." He turned around and behind him was a hammock. He took off his tie and jacket and I had slipped out of my shoes, setting them off to the side of the garden house. He blew out the torches that lit up the small area of the gazebo. Then taking my hand and we sat down in the hammock together, my feet dangling off the ground and his feet keeping us upright.

"I don't get it?" I said as I looked around at the fabric bed-swing, wondering if I was missing something.

Then the next thing I knew he lifted his feet off the ground, and the hammock went flying through the air. As the hammock jolted forward, we were both thrown onto our backs. I let out a small gasp as the light breeze blew over my face. I lay close to him still feeling the slight tingle of the adrenaline that had begun to rush through my body.

We gazed into each other's eyes as the hammock drifted back and forth, slowly coming to a stop. Then his eyes went from mine, straight up to the ceiling. I turned to see what he was looking at, and once again gasped in exhilaration. Just as I thought the night couldn't get any more amazing, I was stunned at the breath-taking sight before me. The ceiling of the gazebo was made of glass. Beyond the glass were the bright twinkling stars in the night sky, dancing and in the spotlight of the moon.

I knew that I had seen the stars before but for some reason in this moment I felt like I was looking at the world for the first time, looking at the night sky for the first time. Then the hole that had formed in my heart from being betrayed by a man I thought loved me seemed whole again, and I could breathe easy knowing that this was right.

Chapter

XIII

We lay snuggled up together in the hammock gazing up at the stars for what seemed like the first time. I found myself cuddling up closer against his chest, with his arm around me. Feeling so comfortable and safe here with him, but somehow there is still a part of me that is still questioning the match. Turning away from the view of the night sky to Sebastian, who was grinning at me.

"What?" I asked softly, trying hard to resist the draw I felt to his lips.

"Nothing, your just so beautiful in this moonlight."

"Thanks." I said with a smile feeling my cheeks get warm. "This night has been amazing. One of the best I have experienced in a long time. It is almost too good to be true." Suddenly feeling something in my gut, not sure what it was trying to tell me. I sat up and began climbing out of the hammock. I walked to the edge of the gazebo, my bare feet clapping the cold wooden floorboards of the tiny garden house. Looking around at the courtyard and the beautiful Mansion that stood erect before me. Trying hard to place this new feeling I just got in my gut, thinking it to be disbelief and that this amazing night couldn't be real.

"What just happened?" Sebastian inquired from behind me still sitting in the hammock. I turned to look at him, only to see him grinning and his eyes twinkling at me like they always did, and he looked so gorgeous. Too gorgeous. So, I turned back to the courtyard and closed my eyes, expecting to wake up from dreaming at any moment.

I stood waiting, then I felt something cold and soft touch my shoulder, sending chills down my spine. I shivered as it slowly drifted down my arm. I turned to find Sebastian standing behind me caressing me with his fingertips.

"This can't be real." I whispered aloud, as his face leaned in closer to mine.

"Why not?" He asked tempting me with his luscious lips. Trying hard to focus on what I was feeling, fighting through the temptation, but being drawn to him anyway. I leaned my head slightly back and closed my eyes eagerly waiting to taste his kiss once more. Then snapping back to reality, I opened my eyes and took a few steps back from his alluring presents. Trying to create some distance but mostly room to think. Feeling the gut feeling suddenly getting stronger, I tried hard to decipher it quickly, so I knew what decision to make and stop ruining the mood of my night with Sebastian.

"Something is wrong?" I whispered aloud to myself, hoping that hearing the words would help me figure out what this new feeling in my gut could be. Trying hard to figure out why my gut was suddenly trying to tell me something it had never before. Just a moment ago the mood of the night was filled with nothing but romance, and now I am having strong feeling in my gut, and I can only assume that it is because something is wrong.

"You'd be surprised what could be real." He said interrupting my inner monologue, stalking toward me slowly, tempting with his eyes me once more. Walking backward and fighting through the attraction, wanting nothing more than to understand why I was suddenly uncomfortable. Trusting my instincts that were screaming something new and unfamiliar, something I couldn't help but think because something was wrong.

I began looking around at where I was, starting to panic as I looked at him coming at me like a carnivorous tiger about to leap on its kill. Why was he suddenly looking at me like that? There is no way this guy is the same guy who I just had dinner with. Lost in my own head, I realized I had lost track of the situation and I began feeling afraid of him.

Sebastian still looking at me like a hungry carnivore I suddenly realized I was alone with a complete stranger. If only I knew what my gut was trying to say. Then I would know what to tell him, and I could know it's alright to give into his charming demeanor. Maybe I wasn't ready to start dating again and that is what my gut was trying to say. Right now, all I know is that the guy in front of me was scaring me to death and I need to get out of my head so I could figure out why he suddenly looked like he might eat me.

"What are you talking about?" I finally said as I backed into the side rail of the gazebo. Sebastian still coming toward me, then stopping abruptly so he was standing just a few feet from me. His demeanor softening from hungry predator to pleading prey.

"There are things in the world that are more real than you could ever believe. It seems too good to be true I know, but you know more about it than you think you do. I know it seems to unreal now, but I also know that inside of you there is a spark that is beckoning to you. Telling you that being here with me is right. I need you to believe me when I say there is no one else I would rather be here with."

"How could you know that? You barely know me." I said still feeling unsure about how I felt and even more unsure if I should trust him after he frighten me just moments ago. I was not going to let his new demeanor fool me back into his arms, something was different about him. It was like my instincts new him to be this predator before I did. Course all I could see before were those sparkling eyes of his. Now I am seeing the truth. Right?

"I know you better than you think I do." He said convincingly.

Then there was a moment of silence we stood staring at each other both of us unsure of what the other would to do next. My head began to pound, trying hard to quickly reason with the situation at hand. What did he do that I missed, that suddenly makes me feel afraid? Can I really trust what he says? Or is he just trying to lure me in just to hurt me?

Then he slowly took a small step in my direction. I flinched and my whole body stiffened. He quickly raised up his hands up, palms outward with his fingers spread. Like I were a small rabbit he was trying not to startle, then he took another small step toward me.

"What are you doing?" I asked, my voice shaking with every word. Knowing that I didn't want to be close to him until I was sure he wouldn't hurt me.

"I just want the night to go back to the way it was." Sebastian said pleadingly, "It was going so well. Don't you think? Then it changed on us and I just want to talk.

"Talk about what?" I said as I started scaling the side of the gazebo, moving slowly against the railing away from him.

"Talk about why you have nothing to be afraid of. Why you can trust me. Why this is more real than anything you've ever experienced in your life."

"I don't understand what you mean."

"Please Jezebel, take my hand. Then we will sit and talk about everything. It is time you knew the truth." I ignored everything he was saying feeling trapped in my own thoughts and feelings, trying to assess the situation. Simultaneously making sure I didn't let him come near me until I knew what to do.

I looked at him, he was so soft and so angelic looking, but my every instinct was still telling me to snap out of it and run for the hills. Torn between what my own instincts were telling me and someone who I just met. Should I, could I trust him? I mean if he wanted to hurt me he would have done it by now, right? Or should I continue to trust my instincts on this one and run. Then I could figure things out later.

I owe it to myself not to gamble my heart away again. I could feel my heart scrunching up inside me just thinking how this amazing guy could be the one to love me, dangerous or not. And with that feeling I felt tears began to run down my face. I didn't know how someone who made me feel so good, could suddenly make me feel so afraid. He didn't look dangerous, but I couldn't shake this strange feeling. And the way he looked at me a bit ago, it was like he wanted to eat me.

"Sebastian, I think I just need some time to think. Thank you so much for everything but I think I need to go home now." I pleaded to him.

Then he took another step toward me, and in that one step I took my opportunity. I ran behind the hammock and around, then jetted toward the exit of the gazebo. Running as fast as I could manage, my fear and discomfort motivating my feet. I could still feel the tears running down my cheeks and rolling backward to my ears as I ran. I wanted nothing more than to curl back up in my bed.

"No, Jezebel. Please don't go." I heard him yell as I made my get away. But my mind was made up, so I continued running.

I barely made it to the steps at the front of the gazebo before I felt Sebastian take hold of my forearm with such force and momentum, it jerked me backwards onto my ass. I looked up to see his face, he still had a hold on my arm, tears were running down my face. For the first time since I had met him his eyes no longer twinkled like honey-ambers. Instead, they were a glowing blood red. They stared into me with such a frenzy it almost burned.

Then my mind drifted back to the eyes I saw my nightmare, and the experience Ashton and I had in the parking garage. I grimaced with fear, realizing the eyes were the same as the ones staring into me right now. The expression on his face was that of a monster, a ferocious killer. Large fangs were coming out of his mouth.

I began squealing and pulling on my arm trying hard to break free. He snarled and growled at me and it was complete certain now that the guy who I had been with the whole night was now gone and some greater being had taken over. I began pulling harder and working my way to my feet.

Then as I was half-way off the ground, he suddenly hurled me out of the gazebo. I hit the ground hard sliding across the gravel, hearing my dress tear and pebbles scattering everywhere. My instincts were now telling me something new but this time it was very clearly telling me to run. So, with little to no hesitation I started to get up, I had to push myself up with my arms because one of my legs had gotten scrapped up and was bleeding profusely. I was in a downward dog position, when I felt a sudden gust and was blasted through the air again. This time landing in one of the many hedges of the labyrinth. Army crawling out from between the branches dragging my legs behind me. I could feel the sharpness of the branches scraping against the skin of my face and arms as I crawled. One of the branches lashing my face deeply along my cheek bone. Finally emerging from the hedge, looking up to find Sebastian standing above me, snarling like a rabid animal. How did he get to me so fast I was clear across the courtyard? He grabbed me by my shoulders and lifted me clean off the ground. He opened his mouth and moved in like he was going to bite me.

"Sebastian please!" I begged, and with those words he paused. Then he shook his head as if shaking himself awake. His eyes flapping open and shut, as they changed from glowing blood red back to the charming amber brown.

"Sebastian?" I said his name again, through sobs of fear and pain. He looked at me and dropped me, my leg being too weak to catch myself I dropped to the ground. He took a few steps back, evidently disturbed at what he saw. I curled up and continued crying, I shivered in the night air. Feeling stupid for doubting my own instincts and not being able to see how dangerous he was sooner. Then I looked up at Sebastian who was scanning me with his eyes. I could see a single tear rolling down his face, and there was nothing, but shame written all over it.

I had cuts on my arms and face from the branches and a giant laceration in my thigh and a few bruises all over my body. Adrenaline still pumping in a state of fear, I began trying to get up listening to the instincts that were still telling me to run. But I slipped on a puddle of my own blood that had formed on the ground beneath me. And for the last time that night I fell hard onto the ground of the courtyard.

Rolling onto my back to look up at Sebastian who was now standing over me, he became a blur and my eyes drifted to the night sky. I lay on the ground looking up at the stars, if they were to be the last thing I was going to see, then that would be alright. So, I closed my eyes half expecting the angel of death to come swooping down and tear away my soul.

Chapter

XIV

I waited to be taken away, slowing coming to terms with death and that this is when my life was to end. I began reflecting on my life and pondering if there was anything that I would do differently.

"Jezebel?" I heard a voice say my name. I took a deep breath and listened and in my mind's eye I saw my brothers and I playing in the back yard.

"Jezebel!" my little brother Tanner called out. Then I chased him and my older brother Charlie, as the leaves of the cottonwood trees blew in the breeze.

I saw us laughing and playing in our backyard; Tanner, Charlie, and I being kids and having fun with the dried leaves. Then I saw my mother and father, join in on the fun as the sun began to set on the horizon. A vison of orange and red, blurring away to a different vision of Ashton sitting on the loft floor. Just the two of us drinking hot cocoa and laughing, and my heart felt warm and so blessed by all the people I had in my life.

Then I saw Michael and all the times we had spent together. For the first time since the breakup, I finally forgave him for hurting me. I didn't feel any more pain just love and gratitude. For the first time in a long time, I was able to play through all the memories of Michael. I saw us on our first date at the ice cream parlor. I played through the many memories like a slide show in my head, then something strange began to happen.

The visons started to change on me again into flashes of something else, something I had never seen before. I was walking down a dark stone hallway with a fiery torch lighting my way. Then as I came to the end of the hallway there was a door with light shining out from underneath. I blew out the torch and pushed the door open. I shielded my eyes with my hand to block the light that was escaping through the doorway. The light began bellowing down into the hall behind me. My eyes began to adjust as I stepped into the room. I stood on a balcony above the main floor, a set of stone steps to my right that lead down to the main room. Slowing, I leaned over the banister to see what was down in the room. Shocked into a state of sheer horror by what I saw. I let out a loud gasp and unexpectedly sat straight up in a bed.

Confused by the abrupt change in scenery I began looking around I realized I was sitting in a dark room, in a bed. Relieved at the realization it was only another nightmare, I did more investigating on the room. The room was lit only by a single flame lantern that sat across from me on a dresser. I looked around the room. I was in a giant bed with lots of pillows and white linens. I was wearing a white sleeveless nightgown, and my hair had been let down from its bun. I tried to remember how I got here, thinking back to the events leading up to the moment I got in this bed. But all I could remember was having dinner with Sebastian, and a romantic evening in the courtyard. Everything after that was a blur; I had no idea what had happened just before I blacked out. I saw nothing in my mind's eye between our romantic tryst in the gazebo and this bed I was in. I did however have a bad feeling in my gut when I tried to fill in the blank space in my mind. Just to be sure I wasn't in another bad dream; I began to patting my upper torso. Making sure that this was my real body, and I was still in the physical world.

Frantically moving my arms up and down my upper body, I felt something tugging on my left arm. I looked down to find I had an IV needle in my arm attached to a bag filled with blood that was hanging on an IV pole beside the bed. Confused why I would need a blood transfusion I began doing a self-evaluation of my body for injuries. I discovered I had a bandage on my left arm, and one on my right thigh, and felt minimal pain. I looked around the room to see if anyone else was present, I couldn't see much through the pale light coming from the lamp. So, I went back to examining the needle in my arm. Figuring out the best way to remove it and I notice there was a small tube attached to the IV beside the one that was administering the blood.

"That is for the morphine," I heard a familiar voice say. Startled by the sudden presence in the dark room I jumped with a huff and began to examine the room once more.

"Who is there?" I said shakingly, I heard no response. So, I prompted the question again but this time more firmly. "Who is there?" I still heard no answer, so I went back to trying to get the needle out of my arm. Then the voice spoke again from amongst the shadows.

"I wouldn't do that if I were you!"

"Well, you're not me!" I blurted back as I picked at the tape on my arm.

"Jezebel!" The voice shouted angrily followed by a slight growl. I let out a small squeal by the inhuman sound that seemed to echo through the area. I slowly pressed the tape back down to please the entity in the room. "Jezebel, please you have lost a lot of blood and you need to rest if you hope to get better." The voice said in an apologetic tone. +

"Where am I? And who are you?" I prompted the voice for answers. Wanting to fill in the blank space in my mind and set my mind at ease.

"You already have all the answers you need. For right now what you really need is to rest. So, please lay back and let the medicine do its job."

Gradually laying back, I rested my head against the headboard. Looking into the shadows to see if I could see who I was talking to. Slowly scanning the room with my eyes to see if I could find any clues in the room that would reveal where I was. At the foot of the bed sat the dresser with the lantern. Then to my far right, against the wall, there was what seemed to be drapes. Beside the bed to my direct right, I saw bottles of morphine, a syringe and bandage supplies as well as a glass of water, on a nightstand.

"I really am thirsty, and I can't quite reach that glass? Could you help me?" Then in the mist of the shadows I heard a rustling, then peeking out of the edge of the shadows I saw shoes. I followed them up the dark figure the faint outline of a man's face.

"Sebastian?" I said anxiously, unsure if I wanted the answer. As the figure took one step out from the shadows my body solidified, and I began to brace myself for the truth. The dark figure became consumed by the faint light of the lamp I held my breath and turned away. I heard the footsteps approach the bed and I turned back to face him. It was Sebastian now in full color and looking at me with a pleasant soft expression and forgiving eyes.

He grabbed the glass off the night table and handed it to me. I looked at it swallowing hard, then wincing at the pain of my dry mouth and throat. I reached for the cup our fingertips brushed against each other, and my mind drifted back to what I saw in my nightmare before I woke up. In my mind's eye I saw Sebastian covered in blood with a ferocious snarl on his face, holding a corps in his arms. His red eyes were staring at me with blood lust, a sight so horrible I once again gasped. Drawing my mind away from that dreadful sight and back to reality, I pulled my hand away from his and looked up at him.

He was standing over me looking at me with his sweet demeanor, still offering me the glass of water. Finding it hard to believe that someone so angelic looking could ever be dangerous, buy still feeling something warning me of the risk that could be hidden beneath his sweet exterior. Even still I was so parched, and he didn't seem to be dangerous currently, so I reached out and pulled the glass back quickly and began chugging down the water. It took only a matter of seconds until it was empty, then I steadily handed the empty glass back to Sebastian.

"Thanks," I said softly as he sat the glass down gently on the nightstand.

"Your welcome," he responded calmly.

"So now that I know who you. Are you gonna tell me where I am? And how I got in this bed?" I said feeling a little more comfortable. My mind at ease seeing a familiar face and pushing back the paranoia and replacing it with the giddy feelings that always accompanied Sebastian's presents.

"We are still at the manor. You fainted, so I carried you inside and had one of my maid's bathe you and dress your wounds. I have been sitting here impatiently waiting for you to wake."

"Wait. Did you say bathe?"

Then he let out a slight chuckle, "Ah, don't worry it was a sponge bath. Your virtue is still intact."

His comment made me blush, but still I felt comforted by his answer. "Did you really bring me inside?" I pondered, baffled by the concept of such chivalrous act being carried out for my sake.

"That is correct." He stated proudly and just.

"Why?" I asked, realizing that no matter how much I want to block out the paranoia, it would be completely irresponsible to do some entirely. So, with the last and only image I had from last night; an image of Sebastian staring at me with a monstrous expression, blood red eyes, and pointy fangs hanging out of his mouth. I inquired to him to fill in the blanks, no matter what the answers may be. I am not a little girl and I need to stop running scared like one.

"I don't quite understand what you mean?"

"Why did you bring me inside instead of," I paused and swallowed hard determined to find my answer I finished confidently, "killing me?"

"Jezebel, I don't wish to kill you!" He said the words with such composure and compassion, that seems to melt away as fast as it appeared. He got up off the bed and began to pace in a small circle, running his fingers through his dark flowing hair. Then he returned to the bedside and looked me in the eye and took a deep breath and said. "I have to apologize to you. I should have controlled myself better and tried harder not to scare you away."

"Well, I think I might have scared myself first. Everything was so wonderful and amazing, but I had just recently gotten out of a relationship with another guy. I am having feelings I have never felt before, feelings I don't yet understand, and it might be because it is too soon for me to date, but I am not sure. I tried to quickly figure it out last night, so I didn't ruin things between us but only got more mixed up. Then in the midst of sorting my thoughts and feelings you suddenly became someone new, someone scary. I was frightened and confused unable to have a moment to collect my thoughts. But then you…" I paused unable to finish the words, cringing at just the thought of them.

"I know. I did, and I am sorry." He said finishing my thought for me and responding accordingly then he continued. "You mean so much to me Jezebel, and I know we just met, and I am trying hard to steadily introduce you to my world. Hoping and praying to the Fates that I don't scare you away. I think I got overwhelmed by your reaction, unsure of what you were think or feeling. I thought was losing you already and I lost control."

"What exactly happened? I'm still a little fuzzy on some of the details?" I questioned.

"I'm afraid if I tell you, then you may run away and never come back."

"That's not an answer, I don't remember much past the moment when we were running toward the gazebo. I was hoping you could help me, so I can better separate my dreams from the truth."

"It was like you said, you got overwhelmed with bliss and began to doubt the moment at hand. You seemed so lost in thought, and I only wished to put your mind at ease so we could continue out lovely evening."

"No, I remember that part, fast forward a little, and I wouldn't say it was bliss."

"Then what would you say it was, ecstasy." He said smoothly, his eyes twinkling like they always do.

"No! I wouldn't say it was anything." I said defensively with a slight grin momentarily forgetting the fear I was just feeling. Relieved that we were breaking through the tension. "Now continue, tell me what happened."

"You began to run away, and I got scared that I might never see you again, so I grabbed your arm." I looked down at my forearm as he said the words and saw the bruises that formed almost a complete handprint. I could make out exactly where his fingers were, I traced them with my finger. Then he obscured the view of the markings on my forearm by covering my hand with his. I looked up into his sweet angelic eyes, he pulled his hand back and he continued his story.

"Then you began to struggle, and I couldn't resist the temptation. A sort of frenzy started to take hold of my mind, and it lives for the thrill of pain and panic. Then after I shook myself back into my right mind, I realized the damage had already been done." Then he looked away his head hanging down, "I was ashamed of what I had done, I am ashamed. Please Jezebel forgive me."

"I still don't even know what I should be forgiving you for. What do you mean when you say, 'a frenzy takes over'? What sort of a frenzy do you mean? What did you do to me?"

"Do you remember anything of what happened? Based on what I just told you, is anything coming back to you?"

"Not really, I do remember you grabbing my arm, and the way you looked at me, but past that my mind is blank."

Then he looked away and took a deep breath. "Just tell me what you think you remember."

"Like I said, I remember you grabbing my arm when I tried to run away, and I remember I looked at you, and your…"

"My what, it's okay you can say whatever you want, even if you think it sounds mad."

"Your eyes, they were blood red and they looked like they were glowing." He stood up and began to nervously pace, "What is it, what did I say?" I asked him anxiously.

"I think that is enough for now you really need to get some sleep." He began tucking me in bed.

"No, Sebastian! That is not good enough, answer me?" I begged as he walked across the bottom of the bed and into the darkness. I heard the turning of the doorknob and saw a quick flash of light coming from the hall, then he disappeared closing the door behind him.

"What have I gotten myself into?" I said aloud to myself as I sat alone in the dark room. I rest my head back against the headboard and watched the flame of the lantern dancing inside its glass chamber. I thought about everything that he told me and how it seemed to match up with my nightmare, and yet I didn't feel afraid anymore. Suddenly my mind felt better knowing that it was possible, and maybe the fear of my nightmare only existed because I thought it wasn't real. I thought I was insane for feeling drawn to such a horrific sight, but now with the little Sebastian has told me I feel confident knowing it could be real. I only needed his verbal confirmation.

I was going to make him tell me the truth, I needed to know. After what he has put me through, he was going to have to face me, and I wasn't going to be afraid this time.

I grabbed the bandage materials off the nightstand and placed them on my lap. I slowly peeled up the unstuck end of the IV tape and ripped it completely off. Then I took the gauze from my lap and tore off a piece of medical tape. Placing the gauze on my arm, I gently pulled the needle out from under it. Then swiftly placed the tape down, strapping the gauze in place.

I rubbed my arm as it adjusted, wiggling my fingers, and getting my blood flow back to normal. I crawled out of the bed, and steadily propped myself on one leg, steadily putting pressure on the other. I began moving along the bedside as my legs started to get used baring my weight. I walked in the direction Sebastian had left the room, my hands stretched out in front of me, searching for the wall at the other end of the room. I finally found it, I moved my hands along the wall to the left finding what seemed to be some sort of closet or wardrobe. Tracing my way back to the wall and making my way to the right until I felt the door. Feeling my way down the door until I found the knob.

"Sebastian?" I growled as I tore the door open. I stepped out into a long hallway that stretched in both directions. It was perfectly lit, and I foresaw no trouble making my way from here. Looking both ways trying to figure out the best way to go and without reason, decided to go right. I hobbled down the hall as quickly as I could, coming to a cross in the hall. I could continue straight ahead or change direction and go to the left or to the right. I frantically studied which direction I wanted to go and something inside me told me to go right. I turned the corner and made my way down the hall screaming his name the entire time.

"Sebastian! Sebastian, I need to talk to you!" I made it to the top of a set of stairs. I looked at the dozens of steps as if some impossible feat, considering my condition they might as well be. Irregardless, I took the first step with my injured leg and then my good one followed. I barely made it down three steps when Sebastian came up behind me shouting.

"What the hell do you think you're doing out of bed!" startled I suddenly lost my footing and tumbled down the steps to the landing that joined the staircase just opposite. I sat up feeling a little lightheaded as Sebastian rushed to my aid. He began examining me for injuries and checked the ones that I already had.

"Why does one of us always end up getting hurt when we are together?" I said looking into his eyes as he lifted me from the ground and carried me up the stairs.

"Just lucky I guess," he said with a grin, "well at least now we are even."

"You didn't need hospitalization when I hurt you." I said a little pouty.

"Well, I am not as fragile as you are."

"I suppose you are right." Then looking around, I noticed he was carrying me back down the way I had come. "Where are you taking me?"

"Back to bed."

"No! I am not an invalid."

"Come on now, back to bed for you!" He said not wanting to hear any of my excuses.

"Okay, find I will go back to bed but on one condition. You give me some answers!" He still wasn't fazed by what I said, and I started to grow even more impatient. We made it back to the room and he sat me on the bed. Rolled the IV pole out of the way, opened the top drawer, pulled out a fresh IV needle and tape out of the small baskets that were in the drawer.

"No way!" I shouted folding up my arms and crossing them over my chest. "You're not putting another needle in me until you give me some answers."

"Jezebel, I do not wish to discuss it with you right now. I will eventually, I promise."

"When?" I demanded.

"Eventually." He repeated.

"That's not good enough." I said getting up off the bed and walking out of the room. Then I heard him let out a sigh, then felt him grab my hand pulling me back to the bed. I sat on the bed still waiting for him to start talking.

"Ok, if it means that I get to keep you in my life then I will tell you everything. I will just have trust in what I have with you. Ask me anything and I will give you a straight answer. I do have to warn you that you might not like what some of the answers are."

I looked at him feeling dignified, I tilted my head and began to think of what to ask first. "Do you think I am crazy?" I finally asked.

"No, I don't think you are crazy."

"Then why did you run off when I asked about seeing your eyes glow."

"It has been a long time since I have been able to share my true self with anyone, and now that someone is you. I knew you wouldn't have liked the answer and I know you wouldn't look at me the same way."

"So, they did turn red?" I asked confident about the answer to my words as they escaped my lips.

"Yes, my eyes do turn red when in a frenzy."

"How? And more importantly why?"

"Well due to the sudden chemical change in my body it changes my eye color to intimidate my prey. As well as other physical changes such as sudden increase in strength and endurance and sometimes even my ability to feel things like guilt or reasoning." He said obviously trying to play off how nervous he was by making his answer seem so matter-of-fact in a smart-alecky tone.

"Why does this happen to you? Why does this 'chemical change' occur?"

I probed trying to get him to say what I already theorized about. Then he looked away and took a deep breath.

"Ok before I answer that I have a question of my own."

"It is only fair." I responded feeling assured, I had nothing to hide.

"Do you trust me?" I began to think about the events of the previous night.

"Should I trust you? Hell no! But do I," then I paused and pondered a little longer then gave my answer with certainty, "Yes, I do. I don't know why; I may not remember exactly what happened last night, but I know it wasn't good. I mean I doubt I'm wearing these bandages as a fashion statement. Even still something in me is telling me that you and I, just makes sense. It was instantaneous and recent, a complete flip compared to what I felt previously. It doesn't seem to matter the amount of danger all the signs are point to; I'm drawn to you Sebastian."

"Well, that has certainly mended my doubts about you. So, to answer your question, my eyes glow red because I am a…" then he paused looking unsure of how to say the words.

"Sebastian your scaring me again. Are you trying to tell me you are some kinds of a monster?" Feeling so sure I was ready to hear the answer, I surveyed him further.

"Monster is a strong word, I'm just trying to tell you that I am not, well human." His answer getting warmer to the theory I had in my mind, started to feel a little less sure I was ready to hear his verbal confirmation.

I stared at him without blinking for a long time, trying hard to get the answer I needed I continued to probe him. "If you aren't human, then what are you?" not sure if I was asking because I wanted the answer or because I was so investing in proving my theory. Just as Sebastian began to open his mouth, and I was reminded once more of the vision I saw just before I woke up in bed, and again when I touched his fingers. "Wait! Actually, stop! I would like to go home now. Would that be alright? I think I need some time away to think and rest. I'm not sure I'm…uh, yeah I would just like to go home."

"Yes, that sounds good." He said clearly feeling jilted but trying to play it off. "I will have Jasper bring the car around. I had some clothes picked out for you as well, change and I will see you are safely returned home." Then he left the room leaving me alone again. Then a maid walked in shortly after and handed me some new clothes, my shoes from last night and a bag with my beautiful velvet gown now nothing but tattered fabric. I began to get dressed and immediately began to take advantage of the alone time I had requested.

Even though I knew I wasn't afraid, I want to be able to continue this conversation with zero doubt in all areas. I still needed to think about last night and figure out everything my gut was trying to tell me. I needed to finally be rid of any past relationship trauma, or emotions. I wanted to be sure of my feelings for Sebastian, and know exactly how much I was willing to invest in him.

But most of all I also wanted to decide for myself how I would feel having confirmation of *my theory* about him before it is spoken aloud. I would hate to accuse him of being a monster when it is only my overactive imagination yearning for the impossible.

I made it to the great hall at the front of the house, pulled the front door open I made my way down the stone steps and toward the car, Jasper was holding the back door open for me. I solemnly placed my things in the backseat and was about to crawl in but stopped abruptly. Then turned back to take one finally look, I glanced back at the majestic house. I began wonder of all the secrets it hide just beyond its stone exterior. I looked up to see Sebastian looking down on me from one of the upstairs windows. Then I felt it again, the feeling deep in my gut. A feeling I only seemed to feel for Sebastian, a feeling that I could not wait to decipher. I climbed into the back of the car, and we drove down the driveway and back toward reality.

CHAPTER

XV

Walking through the front door of the apartment, my head spun trying to get a grasp on reality. Having the feeling like I had just woken up from a very realistic and powerful dream. I looked around and I didn't see Ashton anywhere, but just in case she was lurking about the apartment. I moved as quickly and as quietly as I could to the bathroom. I took off the clothes that Sebastian had picked out for me, peeled of the bandages on my arm and thigh and hopped in the shower. I stood in the water completely still, with my arms wrapped around my body. Feeling secure in my familiar surrounding I began let out the tears of every emotion I had felt last night. The deeper into the feeling I got the lowing my body sunk to the ground. First a slump, then a crouch and finally I was sitting on the floor of the tub just feeling the shower water rain down on me as I cried.

I couldn't believe what had happened to me, I felt more in one night with Sebastian than I did in my entire relationship with Michael. I felt the good, the bad, and even the scary. It didn't' feel real, it couldn't be real. The worst part is I would have loved for it to be, but I knew that it just couldn't. Any of it, not the romance, or even the crazy fantasy monster part. I have a normal real life and I have to wake up and get with the program.

Then my tears turned to a slight giggle realizing that I hadn't told myself that since I was a little girl. No since I used to think our mailman, Mr. Harrington, was a werewolf. Turns out he was just really hairy, and workout a lot. So maybe this was the same thing, maybe Sebastian's dark exterior mixed with modern day pop culture's version of love stories, is just making me imagine things.

I knew that Sebastian was different, but this just didn't make sense. Then I thought back the first night I had met him. How charming he was and the way he looked at me with his ghostly pale face. I still don't understand how he disappeared so quickly when I walked away from the bar. Then I thought about everything he had said to me tonight about him not being human, and how he even almost had me believing it. I learn my lesson a long time ago that things like that only existed in books, I took a deep breath and brushed it off.

I tried to distract myself from thinking about it anymore by focusing on my shower. Examining the wound on my arm, it was almost all healed up. Then I looked at the one on my leg, it was still bleeding. I grabbed the washed cloth and soaked it with fresh hot water and gently patted at the wound. I grimaced at the harsh fabric scraping against the tare in my skin. Then trying my best to stand without stretching my wound open too much, I finished my shower.

Then I stepped out and wrapped a towel around myself. I rummaged the medicine cabinet for supplies to re-dress my wounds. Just as I finished, I heard a banging noise and Mojo start barking, I cracked the bathroom door and stuck my head out. The banging continued, and I realized someone was at the door. Then I heard Ashton yell from the other room, "I'm coming!" Opening the door and she aggressively greeted the person. I listened as closely as I could from the gap in the bathroom door. Watching from around the corner by using the mirror that sat straight across from the front door. I could see Ashton's reflection, and barley out in the hallway.

"Hello, is Jezebel here? I need to speak with her." The person spoke from the hallway, and I realized it was Sebastian.

"No, I thought she was with you."

"Oh, uh she was, but my driver dropped her back home about an hour ago."

"Oh, sorry no I haven't seen her."

"Well, will you please tell her to call me."

"Sure thing."

Just then Mojo came over to the bathroom and started barking at me, I checked the mirror. Ashton was looking to see what was getting him all excited.

"Shh, bad dog! Go away!" I whisper yelled at him, shooing him away with my hand, but he continued barking. "Mojo! Shoo!" I checked the mirror, Ashton had continued talking to Sebastian, over Mojo's barking.

"Is there anything else you needed? Or a message you'd like me to pass along." Ashton asked clearly no longer bothered by the dog.

"Just tell her that I hope to see her again and she is welcome to come over anytime she'd like." He said the words sounding more disappointed than anything.

"Yeah, will do and hey I'm sure she'll turn up."

"Thanks." He responded still sounding disappointed, followed by the sound of the door closing.

I stood in the entrance of the bathroom holding Mojo, I was patting his head waiting for Ashton to go back to bed. Not hearing anymore movement I walked out of the bathroom and was immediately brought to a stop. Ashton was standing with her hands on her hips, just outside the door.

"Dog gave me away, didn't he?" I said in a monotone voice, disappointed that she had caught me.

"Yup!"

I scratched Mojos ears one last time then plopped him back on the floor and began walking around Ashton. Trying to make a break for my bedroom before she could start her interrogation.

"Um, excuse me? Did you plan on telling me what the hell is going on?" She said as she chased me across the loft. "Jezebel answer me!"

I made it to the doorway of my bedroom when I finally turned around. "I don't want to talk about it right now but thank you for caring. I will explain everything in the morning." Then I started to close the door behind me, but Ashton stopped it with her hand.

"Jezebel!"

"What do you want?" I said whining, walking into my room toward my dresser.

"Well how about you tell me what happened to your face and arm for starters?" She said grabbing ahold of my head, trying to get a good look at the cut I had along my cheekbone.

"It's nothing alright!" I barked slapping her hands away and then getting my pajamas out of my dresser.

"Then explain to me why you snuck in here? And why Sebastian is at the front door asking you too call him at 3 a.m.?"

"I just got home alright I'd like to go to sleep. I defiantly need time to process things before I can openly discuss it with you." I yelled defensively as I frantically rushed around my room looking for my hairbrush.

"Just tell me what happened tonight."

"I said I will tell you when I understand what it even is that I need to tell you, alright!" I said still searching.

"Alright, but at least tell me what happened to your face? Why you have so many bandages?" She said sounding irritated.

"I scratched it on a branch, alright! Are you happy now?" I asked sarcastically and immediately changing the subject. "Where in goddess name is my brush?" I blurted stomping my foot down.

"Fine I will leave you be, so we can both get to bed but don't think this is the end of this conversation." Ashton said firmly as she walked over to my bedside table and pulled my brush out from behind the lamp. Then walked back to me and handed it to me. Then abruptly turned to leave the room, closing the door as she exited.

I threw my brush on the bed as she left, then plopped down on the foot of my bed. Hunching over with my hands resting on my forehead and took a deep breath. Then once again shook it off, I stood up and got dressed into a tank top and shorts. I began brushing out my long brown hair, I thought about Ashton and how bad I felt about our little tryst while I brushed. It may not have seemed like much, but I wanted to make sure we were on the same page. I braided my damp tangle free hair it into one long side braid.

Then I walked to Ashton's room and lightly knocked on the door.

"Ashton?" I asked quietly and heard no answer, so I knocked once more.

"Come in," I heard her grumble from the other side. I opened the door and walked inside to find her sitting on the bed with her bedside lamp on, bundled up under her blankets.

"Are you sleeping?" I asked slowing making my way into her room.

"Not yet." She replied softly.

"Can we talk?"

"Sure." she said as she sat up in her bed, I took a seat at the bottom of the bed just in front of her and took a deep breath.

"First off, I am sorry for getting angry but if what happened to me is in anyway real, then I might just go into cardiac arrest. I don't know if I should be scared or excited. All I know is if I say it out loud then your gonna think I am crazy. So, I would rather keep it to myself for now; just until I can wrap my head around it and know how I'm supposed to feel about it. I can't tell you much right now okay, but I assure you that I will."

"What about Sebastian?"

"What about him?"

"Did the date go well at least?" she said obviously trying to comfort me by changing the subject.

"Oh yes! We had a wonderful dinner, we talked and laughed so much. It was one of the best nights of my life, but it seemed to change in the blink of an eye. I don't know what it is about him, but you know that feeling I was talking about before, that he makes me feel like no one ever has. Well, I got that feeling and every part of me was thriving on the high, but I feel like I shouldn't. I almost feel guilty for enjoying the feeling I get, like it would make me a bad person or something."

"Maybe it was just your nerves."

"No, it was more of a terror feeling and now I know why but…"

"What do you mean by 'terror feeling'?" she said interrupting me.

"Nothing I'll explain that part later."

"No! Wait, did he do this to you? Did he hurt you?" she said, suddenly startled, scooting closer to me and grabbing my hands. I said nothing, trying my hardest not to answer any questions that would rope me into telling her more than she needed to know. If this is real than I don't want to get Ashton stuck in the middle of it too.

"I'm fine." I said as calmly as I could manage stepping off the bed and walking away a couple of feet. Then I turned to face her again, "Ashton can you just trust me when I say that I am going to be alright."

"I don't know how I can. I see that you are obviously in some kind of struggle. I want to help you, but I don't know how. I don't know what happened to you over the last couple days hours, but I am seriously worried."

"Wait, back up a bit. Did you say *days*?"

"Yeah, you left that night, and then you were gone all of yesterday."

"I seriously need to go to bed, I'm suddenly not feeling so well." I said as I tried to keep from falling over feeling suddenly lightheaded and dizzy.

"Are you alright?" Ashton said jumping out of bed to my side.

"I…I don't know what's happening to me."

"Come on let's put you to bed."

Ashton helped carry me to my room and tucked me into bed. Left the room for a brief moment then returned with a glass of water which she left on the nightstand.

"That was weird and unexpected, maybe it is just fatigue. Try and get some sleep and well see how you feel in the morning." She said sitting on the edge of my bed petting my hair. "And don't worry about telling me about what happened I know you will tell me when you are ready." Then she got up, turned off the lamp and left the room.

I lay in bed feeling woozy and dizzy even while lying down, and everything was blurry. So, I closed my eyes and tried to fall asleep, but it was hard to focus all I could think about was Sebastian. I couldn't help but feel like I wanted to see him. Even after what I knew about him and what he did to me. I still couldn't stay away. What was this feeling? Would it ever go away? But even bigger question was, did I want it to?

Chapter

XVI

I woke up the next morning at 8:30, I sat up to see the sun peaking in through the sliver of an opening left in the door. I climbed out of bed and walked around the house. The only living soul I could find was Mojo who was napping on the living room couch.

I walked into the bathroom to find a note taped to the bathroom mirror, it was from Ashton, and it read, *'Hey hun sorry I missed you, hope you're feeling better will be out all morning. See you after you get home from work-Ash.'*

"Oh shit." I said aloud, realizing that I had to go into the office today. I crumpled the note and through it into the trash can. I turned on the sink letting the water get warm I grabbed the toothpaste as I lifted my hand to take off the cap the toothpaste tube exploded. Squirting all over my hand and dripping on the sink. Disgusted by the sticky mess I tossed the now empty tube in the trash, washed my hands and the sink. Deciding that I would just rinse with mouth wash and call it a day, I finished up in the bathroom.

Just as I was turning to leave the door slammed shut in front of me. Startled I fell onto my ass, I could hear Mojo barking on the other side of the door. I got up and walked to the door, slowly I reached for the knob, turning it slowly. Then in one quick motion I opened the door and without a second thought hurried out of the bathroom into the hallway. Not quite sure what I expected to happen. Standing just in front of the bathroom door I began investigating the entryway. Seeing nothing that would have caused the door to suddenly close. Feeling satisfied in my investigation I moved on, heading into the kitchen for some breakfast.

I placed the tea kettle on the stove and turned it on, as I waited for the water to heat up, I got a mug and some honey. Then I grabbed the bag of blueberry bagels and popped one in the toaster. I pushed the lever down for the toaster to start and it just came right back up, so I tried it a second time then I saw that Ashton must have unplugged it. I grabbed the plug and inserted it into the outlet and out of nowhere my hand was shocked with a jolt of electricity. Then the toaster began to spitting out sparks, and suddenly burst into flames. I quickly unplugged the toaster and was shocked again.

The toaster still engulfed in flames I dropped the plug and quickly grabbed the fire extinguisher from beneath the sink. I put the fire out and then suddenly the kettle began to whistle. I rushed to turned off the stove and grabbed the kettle and the exact second my hand touched the handle it blew its top. Boiling water went bursting everywhere, shouting at the burning sensation on my skin I through the hot tea kettle into the empty sink. Then I stood frozen as the now cooled water mist down on top of me.

I slowly backed out of the kitchen, with my hands raised in front of me trying hard not to disturb anything else. Then as I took a step backward something touched my back. I quickly did a jump pivot to see who or what was behind me and saw that it was only the counter. I let out a sigh of relief and placed my hand over my heart to slow it down.

Just then the clock that hung in the kitchen started to ding, I looked up and saw it was 9 o'clock. I quickly rushed to my room and pulled on some black tights, a long sleeve plum dress, long enough to cover my thigh bandage, and some black boots and was out the door.

I made it to work just ten minutes before I had to clock in, so I made a stop in the lounge to see if there were any scraps of food. I was lucky enough that today someone had brought donuts, so I picked out a couple of cake donuts, filled my tumbler with water and inserted a green tea bag. Then began heading back to my cubical, I sat at my desk to find a manila envelope sitting on the desk. Stamped in big red letters right along the seal were the words IMPORTANT DOCUMENTS.

I looked around to see if there was anyone who could possibly have left it there. Seeing no one, I tore open the seal to find a single piece of paper inside. Which I found strange but slipped the paper out of the envelope and read it to myself quietly.

Dear Ms. Jones,

I regret to inform you that your term of employment at Hourglass Magazine has been terminated, effective immediately. Due to your lack of attendance and commitment to the company. We request that you are logged out of all company computers, phone systems, copiers and/or fax. You have until noon today to clear out your belongings and vacate the premises. If you do not comply, your belongings will be packed up and you will be escorted out of the building by our security team.

We thank you for your service, and cooperation.
Miranda Gills and the
Human Resource Department

I put the letter down on my desk in shock, I looked at the time on the battery-operated clock that sat on my desk it read 9:49 a.m. I hung my head and began thinking. I didn't understand what was happening to me today. Just last week I thought my life was getting better and now things are happening to me that just don't make any sense. The loft basically attacked me this morning and now I don't even have a job.

I walked back to the lounge dragging my feet a little, opened the supply closet and grabbed an empty printer paper box and took it back to my desk. I began to pack up my things, quickly munching on the donuts I snagged as I packed before someone could tell me that I had no right to those either.

Just as I put the last piece of donut in my mouth, I was suddenly startled by Miranda who had popped into the cubical next to me out of literally nowhere.

"So, I see that your almost packed up." She said with a little too much enthusiasm.

"I received your letter, and I am all packed up, but Miranda can I just ask why?"

"I told you that you weren't irreplaceable and yet you still didn't show commitment or even show up here at the office. So, it's toodle-loo for you. Hurry up and pack your things and get out of my department." She said firmly pursing her lips.

"You can't just fire me! I work harder that anyone who actually shows up for work, and I'm a hell of a better writer!" I defended, not even sure why I was defending my position. Not like I liked my job and I thought so many times of quitting that it didn't really bother me that I was let go. I think that it was just Miranda's amount of balls to throw it in my face that got me all revved up.

"You snooze you lose." She said seeming the least bit affected by my defense.

"You know what Miranda seeing as I am no longer an employee. I think it is about time someone took those knock off pumps and shoved them right up your ass!" I don't know where this new courage was coming from, but it felt good. I felt powerful and in charge, it was intoxicating.

"Oh, I am quivering," clearly trying to cover her fear with sarcasm.

Then I took a step toward her, which was way more intimidating that it looked seeing as she was towering over me, she flinched just a little. Then I paused and backed off with a grin and a chuckle.

"You know what, you aren't worth my time. Now thanks to you I don't have to spend any more of my time kissing your boney-barbie ass!" Then I grabbed the box from my chair and placed it on my hip, walking away backwards I took my badge off and as I flicked it on the desk I said, "You will regret the day that you fired Jezebel Jones!"

Then as the badge left my hand the craziest thing happened, it caught on fire. It landed directly on the group a of papers the whole stack of papers burst into flames setting off the emergency sprinklers. Trying hard to hide my astonishment I swiftly turned and walked out of the office, pretending as though I hadn't even noticed the fire or sprinklers.

I quickly made my way to the elevator and frantically pressed the button. Hoping for the doors to closes before someone could catch me. As I rode the elevator to the ground floor I stared at my blurry reflection in the stainless-steel wall of the elevator. I thought to myself. *Did I do that? I did, didn't I? Does that mean that I caused everything this morning in the loft?* I began to feel my stomach clench with fear. I shook it off as the elevator dinged and I stepped out with my box. Speed walking through the lobby and out the door, as confident and innocent as I could manage.

Once outside, I quickly raced to my car not sure what was happening to me, but fairly sure that I started the fire. I sped home trying extremely hard to remain calm and to avoid any more surprises. Finally making it home I burst through the front door practically tripping over myself. I dropped the box on the floor and began staring at my hands like I had never seen them before.

"Hey, I didn't know you were coming home for lunch. I suppose it is for the best. So would you like to explain to me what happened to the toaster?" Ashton said from the kitchen making casual small talk. I ignored her and just dropped to my knees on the floor, breaking down in hysterical tears.

"Oh my, are you alright?" Ashton said as she rushed toward me.

"No! Stop! Stay away from me!" I shouted as she approached me, crawling away from her, tumbling across the floor in tears.

"Okay, but you really need to tell me what is going on now." She said in her mother voice, trying to force me to calm down.

I sat on the floor, my back to Ashton, still staring at my hands trying to figure out how this could be possible. So many things have been happening to me lately, and I didn't understand why. All I could think was; *Why is this happening to me? Am I crazy? There is no way in hell this is really happening! Did this have something to do with Sebastian?*

I combed my fingers through my hair gripping at the roots with both hands, rocking back and forth dissecting my brain for answers. I felt like I was losing my mind. *Was I having a mental break or something? Do I need to be committed? Or was this just my over active imagination?*

Then I heard the floorboard creek behind me. Startled I turned, firing a blast of air from my hands, sending Ashton flying through the air into a wall of photos. Then she dropped to the floor and the broken glass came crashing down on top of her like crystal rain. I jumped to my feet startled at what just happened, looking at my hands again in skepticism. Then I swiftly made my way to my feet I looked at her folded over on the floor.

"Ashton, sweetie? Are you okay?" I asked slowly approaching her waiting for a response, but she didn't move or speak. I didn't even know if she was breathing. I knelt down in front of her holding my breath. I put my finger just beneath her nostrils, then let out a sigh of relief. Then I gently placed my hand on her shoulder and gave her a little shake, praying I wouldn't hurt her again. She finally came too, and I saw that she had a piece of glass in her hand.

"Oh my, Ashton are you okay?" I said feeling so awful and guilty.

"I don't know. What happened?" she said still in a daze.

"I'm not really sure. Let me get something for your hand, don't move." Then I rushed to the medicine cabinet in the bathroom and grabbed some supplies. I exited the bathroom to fine Ashton at the kitchen sink running water on her hand, she had removed the shard of glass.

"Ashton!" I shouted, rushing to the kitchen, and dropping everything on the counter before rushing to her side. "I told you not to move."

She didn't say anything she just stood speechless. I turned the sink off and grabbed the towel I brought from the bathroom and wrapped her hand. I escorted her to the table and sat her down. Grabbing the supplies from the counter and moving them to the table before she could move. Looking at her hand, still bleeding profusely, I began tweezing out the small slivers of glass that were left behind. Then grabbed some alcohol, and poured it over the wound, she didn't even cringe. I wrapped her hand in some gauze and secured it with some medical tape.

"There, that should be good. I don't think it was a big enough piece for you to need stitches. Do you want me to make you something to eat?" I asked in a soft voice, trying to ignore the guilt I felt inside me. She didn't say anything she just sat at the table, holding her now wrapped hand against her chest. I got up from the table and began to walk away when I noticed something shiny in her hair, it was glass. I quickly reached out to grab it and Ashton flinched with such fury she fell out of her chair and onto the floor.

"I'm sorry!" I remarked for touching her in her delicate state without telling her. I loved Ashton to death and the girl was tough as nails when it came to conflict, but in the event of a crisis she was soft like cotton candy.

She curled into a ball on the floor where she landed. In an effort not to make matters worse I left the room and went to cope with the events of the day. After cleaning up the bits of glass and broken picture frames, I went to my studio. I sat down at my desk logged on to my laptop, opened a web browser and began researching the shit out of the supernatural. Including the events that happened this morning and when I was with Sebastian. Hoping that it would make things better if I at least had confirmation for the things that I thought I knew.

CHAPTER

XVII

Sitting at my desk I was clicking on random articles about fantasy lore, monsters, and magic. I loved this stuff and already had a pretty large knowledge base of it but never thought I would ever be researching it for real. That's what Sebastian was talking about right? The night of our date, he was trying to tell me that magic is real. As much as it scared me, part of me (the part that thrived on this stuff my whole life) was screaming with ecstasy.

Even though I had figured it out long ago, I was afraid to admit the truth about what he was, not to myself or to anyone for that matter. Not sure how it would come out, I didn't want to sound foolish. At the same time his new attributes didn't bother me, I wasn't scared of him, nor did I think it to be a problem. I however want to be sure it was factual before I could hear it spoken aloud or say it myself. From the moment I'd set eyes on Sebastian something in me knew that he would change my life; but I never would have guessed it to be like this.

Even with all the research I still had some holes that needed filled. If Ashton was ever going to be able to be near me again without flinching, I needed those holes filled. There was only one place that I knew I could go for the answers, the only problem standing in my way was myself. *Was I ready to admit the truth? Am I ready to confront my fear of sounding insane?* If what I think he said was real, then he is the only other person who I know has the knowledge to fill the gaps and I know he will be able to explain.

I began sneaking across the living room to the door I peeked into kitchen where I had last left Ashton curled up on the floor, but she was no longer there. Assuming she had gone to bed I grabbed my coat and my purse and ran out the door before Ashton could see me.

On the drive over, I began mentally preparing myself for what was to come. This was the day that my life would change forever because I was finally going to admit the truth about what I knew. Turning into the gate and up the driveway feeling my nerves on edge, so I took a deep breath and told myself I was doing the right thing. I got out of the car finding.

89/+-------5 my way throw the night and up the steps, I took another deep breath and knocked. Banging on the giant oak doors screaming Sebastian's name until finally someone answered the door, it was Jasper.

"Hello, what can I do for you Ms. Jones?" Jasper said as polite and creepy as always.

"I need to see Sebastian!" I shouted frantically.

"I'm sorry Madame but the master is busy at the moment. I will have to ask you to come back another time."

"No! Jasper I need to see him now!" I said starting to panic.

"Ms. Jones as I have told you the master is not seeing anyone today," he said in a firm voice.

About ready to give up, I turned slightly away, but something inside me pulled at my instincts. "I'm sorry Jasper." Then I pushed passed him through the door and into the great hall. I immediately ran up the stairs, and up and down hallways, bumping into maids and servants. There was still no sign of him, but that wasn't about to stop me. I was running down a hall about out of breathe, when someone came out of one of the rooms, and the glasses he was holding went crashing to the ground. We both dropped to the ground and began picking up the broken pieces of glass on the ground.

"Oh, I am so clumsy…" I began then I looked up to see that it was Sebastian, "Where the hell have you been?" my mouth blurted without my approval.

"Excuse me?" He said a little shocked by my tone but continued grabbing pieces of glass.

"I have a bone to pick with you!" I said starting to get revved up again.

"So, I gathered," he said in a calm but sarcastic voice.

"Cut the bullshit Sebastian! I know that you know that I know what you are!"

"Come again?"

"I know, dammit!" I screamed at the peak of my anger.

Then finally all caught up he stood motionless, his head hanging and face expressionless. Placing the broken pieces of glass on a nearby table, he grabbed my empty hand. Then he looked at me with sympathetic eyes that jerked at my heart and calming me down.

"Come with me." He said jerking his head behind him, gesturing the direction he wanted to go. I placed my handful of glass next to his and followed him down the hall still holding his hand.

As we walked to the back of the mansion, I followed him as closely as I could to be sure not to get lost as my eyes wondered. The giant windows to my left were beautifully famed with prism glass. The kind that makes colored rays when the sun shines through it. Between each window were long heavy burgundy curtains pulled aside with golden robe. Through the giant window I could see the courtyard labyrinth and far in the distance I could make out the white gazebo. All blanketed by the luminescent glow of the moon. Then as I thought about the memories of the courtyard I cringed and looked back to Sebastian.

We walked down serval hallways and even went up a small flight of stairs, and the decor began giving off a different vibe. It wasn't Hollywood glam anymore, now it felt more like Haunted-wood horror. Finally, we walked to the end of a hallway that had only a bookshelf, I looked around confused. I scanned the hall to see if there was maybe a door that I wasn't seeing.

"Sebastian, I am confused." I said feeling a little anxious.

"Just wait, I will explain everything soon, you have to trust me." The sympathy in his eyes began melting away to only happiness, and he gave me the look a look like he knew something I didn't. Then he turned back to the bookshelf, pulled out one of the books and reached back into its place to the back of the shelf. I heard a clicking noise then suddenly the bookshelf began to move. Shifting from its place in the wall, sinking inward, then sliding off to the left. Standing with my arms wrapped around my chest, my mouth wide open and my eyes bulging. I baby stepped into the newly revealed room, just behind Sebastian. Entering the room, all the wonder from my childhood dreams seemed to come to life.

The entire room was made of the same stone as the rest of the manor, but it was more of a dingy gray color. The entire room was like a giant layered cylinder. The ceiling above us has a giant hole in the middle. Making the second floor form a giant ring around the outside walls of the room. Creating a vaulted ceiling that stretched all the way above the second floor.

Back on the main floor are stone columns, circling all the way around the room supporting the second level ring. With shelves wedged between all the columns filled with books, different sized bottles, and tools. The floor of the main room has a thick ring that circles all the way around the room. Leaving an even lower circle shaped platform in the middle of the room. Finally standing perfectly erect in the middle of the lower platform, was a stone podium with an old dusty book sitting on it. I notice there was stuff on the second floor but there was no staircase or even ladder.

I twirled around trying to see what could be up there through the giant gaping hole in the ceiling. Then I noticed I had been smiling ridiculously the entire time since entering the room. Then floating down from my rush of excitement and wonder, I looked around to find Sebastian. He was leaning against the bookshelf that doubled as the door, which was still moved from the entrance, his arms crossed and a smirk planted on his face.

"This is amazing!" I said with astonishment written all over my face. "How do you get up there?" I asked in kind of a mousy voice as I pointed the second layer of the room.

"Let's not get ahead of ourselves, okay." He said as he peeled himself off the side of the shelf walking toward me. "First, I have to tell you something really important. I am glad you are enjoying yourself though, that's a good sign. Now come with me."

Then he walked to the opposite side of the room, between two of the columns was a door. On the other side was a small room with a rectangular table and four chairs sitting in the middle. There were papers and books covering the table. The wall to our left had a giant red velvet curtain with a golden pull cord. Sebastian grabbed the cord, and then turned to look at me.

Chapter

XVIII

"Okay, are you ready?" He asked me after first taking a deep breath. I said nothing only feeling a slight chill, with the hairs on my arms and the back of my neck standing on end. Sebastian, obviously aware of my concern said, "There is nothing to be afraid of okay. You are safe here."

I shivered and began warming my body back up by rubbing it briskly with my hands. Then with a nod I said, "Okay I am ready. I am not quite sure what I am ready for, but the time is now."

With those words spoken aloud, Sebastian pulled the cord hard. Grunting as he tugged it behind him toward the ground. The velvet curtain began to lift revealing a shocking truth. There behind the curtain was a painting of a woman, a woman who looked exactly like me. I gasped jolting myself backwards in shock, losing my balance in the process and falling to the floor. Having not yet blinked, I stared at her, caressing my own face with my fingertips as I examined her features.

Almost like I was looking in a mirror, expecting to see the movements reflected back as conformation as why I seemed to be seeing myself in the portrait. It was a large old canvas painting with a black carved frame. She was standing kind of sideways with her hands clasped together in front of her. She had her hair up in a bun on the top of her head with loose waves framing the outer part of her eyes. And she was wearing an army green dress, that looked to be centuries old.

"Who is that?" I asked slowly in a hushed voice, still not having taken my eyes off her.

"Her name was Brigitta." Sebastian said as he walked in front of the painting looking up at her with sagging shoulders.

"Who is she?"

"She is you." He said solemnly causing me to gasp once more. Then crawling back to my feet, I walked toward him, standing next to him in front of the giant canvas.

"What do you mean? How can she be me? I am here now."

"Come sit and I will explain."

Then we both walked to the table, and I sat down. I waited patiently as he began rustling through the many papers and books that sat on the table. Finally digging out an old wax tapestry, then climbing up onto the table to sit. He looked it over before finally laying it out in front of me. The wax was cracked, and the tapestry was an old dingy yellow, but you could still make out what was on it.

In the middle of the textile there was a black star with a compass whitened out in the middle of the shape. Then there was a circle encompassing the star. Then at the tip of each point of the star was a box with words in it, but the words were in a different language. The letters looked like something I had seen before, but I couldn't quite put my finger on it. Then in bold letters at the top were the words, *Pente Stadia Thanatos.*

I traced over the words with my fingers, feeling its rough texture beneath my fingertips. Then Sebastian began to speak up.

"Pente Stadia Thanatos." he said pronouncing the words that were underneath my fingers. I looked up at him a little confused then he continued. "It means five stages of death. That is why you and Brigitta look the same, you are the same person."

"How can that be?" I said still slightly confused.

"Okay so let me explain this, this system has five fates, they symbolize the five points on the star." He said as he pointed to the five-different boxes on each point of the star. "Each fate plays a singular role in the greater scheme of the universe. Their job is to keep the balance of the death cycle amongst all supernatural beings. However, some souls are defective and are defiant to life in the natural world. These people are called Ainigma. They are then either recycled and placed back into the system with a new life, or they are sent to purgatory to burn."

"Wait, they burn?"

"Yes, I am afraid. If the Fates rule that an Ainigma's soul is beyond repair, they destroy it forever."

"Oh my, that is terrible! How do they decide?"

"Well, each of the five fates is in control of a different part of the cycle." Then pointing to the box on the head of the star and working his way around to each point in a clockwise rotation, he explained. "The first is Krisi the Fate of Judgement, she is the sole decider of whether or not a soul is to be recycled or sent to purgatory. Next is Anakyklono and he is the fate of reincarnation, and he is charge of a soul's new placement and role in the natural world depending on if they are a recycled soul or reborn. Then there is Ponos and Penthos, pain and mourning. They are not only the only fates who are involved with the living and the dead. But they are also the only two who really don't serve a purpose without the other. Finally, we have Parasma the fate of Passage, she is the key holder of the gates of the spirit world. She opens the passage that leads to the natural world to begin the journey of rebirth or to purgatory where you burn."

"So, when do you know if you get recycled?"

"Well, every soul is surveyed at the end of its twenty-fifth year, and if it is an Ainigma it gets recycled. If not, then it is allowed to live out its life and to have a natural death before being reborn."

"How is it that no one knows about these so-called, fates?"

"Well, there aren't very many supernatural beings in the world anymore, and the ones who are still out there live in the shadows. And since the cycle doesn't apply to humans, it's not really something that has been passed down in the mortal world."

"Then how is it that you know all about them?

"Well, my kind is included in this system."

"Wait, your kind?" I said trying my best to make it seem as if I had no idea what he was talking about, as if to persuade him to confess it aloud.

"Yes, because of what I am. You said that you knew!"

"Knew what?" I said, keeping up my act of innocence.

Then jumping off the table in a bit of a panic he began interrogating me. "Jezebel, just a moment ago when we ran into each other in the hall you yelled that you knew the truth! Were you referring to something else?" I didn't say anything just stared at him with a blank expression and waited for him to speak. "Jezebel do you know the truth or not?"

"The truth about what?" I said with a bit of a conniving grin.

"About what I am?"

"I don't know. What are you? I want to hear you say it, out loud."

Then as he caught on to my little act, he locked his jaw and scowled at me. Trying hard to fight the dimples in his cheeks, that were trying hard to make their way through his invisible grin. Then straight faced and confident he said aloud. "I, Sebastian Adrian Markus Baldovino am a vampire from the Sapphire clan." Then there was a brief pause, and I was stunned into silence, having heard the words spoken aloud for the first time made me feel more surprised than I thought they would. We looked at each other and his dimples seemed to disappear completely and there was no longer an apparent hidden smile. Just a devilish snarl as he continued speaking. "Are you afraid?"

Then he stared me down, and my eyes began to burn like the other night when he had attacked me. But I searched deep inside myself, the truth began to fight to the surface, this was the part of me that would not be silenced by his animal stare again.

Then I climbed to my feet, standing tall and confident I leaned into him, so my nose was touching aligned with the tip of his and matching up our gaze. I gritted my teeth and said with a strong powerful voice said, "No! I Jezebel Selene Jones am not afraid of you!"

"Good, because I will never hurt you again. You have my word." He said as he placed his arm out in front of him, parallel to his chest and bowed his head.

"What was that?" I said a little freaked out by his weird gesture, sitting back down in my chair.

"That is a symbol of respect but is more often used when one makes an oath to protect another. I am vowing to never bring harm to you or to let another harm you."

"I trust you."

Then he sat in the chair next to me, we stared at each other in adoration for a couple minutes. Until my cheeks began to feel warm, and I had to turn away from his dazzling amber eyes. Then he scooted his chair closer to me and brought the attention back to the tapestry.

"So, because I am a, a"

"You can say it, I told you I am not afraid. I don't' know why because I have seen firsthand what you are capable of doing. Yet for some reason the only thing I feel when I am next to you is safe and warm." I said smiling in a soft encouraging voice, and he smiled back at me.

"Because I am a Vampire, myself and others like me hardly ever die we are a bit of an exception to this system."

"So, what does that make me?"

"You, precious Jezebel, are the recycled soul of my departed love Brigitta." He said as he softly touched my cheek with his palm, and then looking back at the painting on the wall.

"But you said the only souls that get recycled are the, what did you call them, ainig…"

"Ainigma. Yes. Her soul, the same one that is yours now, was reluctant to fulfill her destiny. You see you're both something much greater than just mere humans."

Knowing exactly what he was talking about, I looked down at my hands, remembering what had happened at the loft, at the office and what I did to Ashton. I closed my palms holding my hands to my chest looking away from Sebastian, ashamed. Then with his finger bent below my chin, he began lifting my face to meet his.

"You need not be embarrassed of yourself, or your great skill. You, sweet Jezebel, are a witch." Then he lowered his hand and walked over to stand in front of Brigitta. "You both were."

"I am a witch?" I asked myself in a whisper.

Then from the shelf next to the painting of Brigitta. Sebastian grabbed an old small wooden box and carried it to the table. Then opening the box, he pulled out another old, faded piece of parchment, unfolded it and laid it on top of the wax tapestry. It had Old English style words on it and at the bottom there was what seemed to be signatures, each next to a wax seal. One was blue wax with a capitol B and the other red with a capitol S, the signatures were both in a faded burgundy red color. I traced my finger over the names trying to make out the letters.

"What is this?" I asked as I gave my full attention back to Sebastian.

"This is the treaty of our ancestors, now that you understand the system, it is time for you to learn about the treaty. A long time ago there were two separate covens, one was the vampire coven of Baldovino, my ancestors. Then the other was the witch coven of Sanballet, your ancestors. The two covens were always at odds with each other, being both monsters that take human form.

This feud continued for centuries, until one day the king of the Sanballet coven came to my ancestors pleading for help for his only daughter Malishca, who was dying. She was not only his heir, but also, she meant the world to him. He surrendered to the King of the Vampires, offering they make a pact in exchange for their help. So, both kings went to the temple of the Fates to bargain her life. The great Warlock told the Fates that he would offer to share the power and abilities of his coven to the clan of Baldovino, only if they shared in their immortality so that his daughter may continue living.

The Fates drew up this treaty agreement and made both Kings sign it in their own blood. Then told the Vampire king to bring forth his oldest son, the vampire prince does so. The fates then instructed him lay next to the weary body of Malishca, he does accordingly. The Fates then ripped out the son's soul and tore it in half, and before either coven could retaliate. The Fates took a strand of stars from the sky and began weaving two new halves to the soul and placing one in each of the bodies. Binding them as eternal soul mates. As long as they find each other and complete the bond, no matter the generation, both clans will share in the other clan's abilities." Then he paused and started to look sad and continued. "Brigitta broke the cycle before we had a chance to make the bond and was recycled."

"What did she do that was so bad?"

"It was not so much that she did something bad. The fates just branded her as an Ainigma. You see there is a predestined path in life. They are given the free will to find that path in their own time, the important part is that they eventually find the path and they show no resistance to following it. The thing about Ainigma's is they aren't fulfilling their predestined place in the world. They are fighting against the very life chosen for them. Brigitta struggled to follow her path and the life chosen for her, she wanted something else."

"So, since Brigitta's soul was recycled what does that mean for the bond of the covens."

"You didn't think we met by pure coincidence, did you?"

"Actually, yeah I kind of did." I said with a little bit of a giggle. Then he smiled at me and offered me his hand. I took it and he began leading me out of the room back to the layered chamber we had come from, talking the entire way.

"Each coven was given a gift from the Fates to signify the unity and the joining of the clans. So that each generation could form the bond of souls. The clan of Baldovino was given a grimoire and the coven of Sanballet was given a sapphire amulet." Then we stood on the outer ring of the first floor just in front of the podium. "This is the Grimoire of Sanballet, that was given to my family generations ago. It was given to us so that my family may know the spells that were shared between the clans."

I looked at the old brown leather book that sat atop the stand. It was quite large, and it had a thick leather band that was wrapped all the way around it sealing it shut, that meets on the top. Connecting each end of the band was a giant buckle that clicked close to seal the book. The buckle that joined the bands was in the shape of a golden sun decorated with tiny rubies. Then on the right side of the sun, there was a hole in the shape of a crescent moon, like there was a piece missing.

"Why is there a hole in the buckle?" I asked Sebastian curiously.

"That is where the Sapphire amulet, that was gifted to the clan of Sanballet, joins together with the Grimoire to symbolize the bond."

"Well, where is it?" I asked anxiously.

"No one has seen it for years. Since Brigitta was recycled and we didn't know how many years it would take for her to come back to us. The Sanballet coven were no longer joined together with the Baldovino clan. So, the witches lost their immortality and the remaining members dwindled down over the years. And without the use of magic the vampire clan was no longer feared by the humans and became easy targets. We were hunted by the humans for sport, granted we weren't helpless animals. But we couldn't defend ourselves as well as we could with magic. Most of the clan was wiped out alongside the witches. What was once a great empire is now in ruins."

"Wait I thought vampires were immortal?"

"Yes, meaning we live a long time but that doesn't mean we can't be killed. Granted we are basically born dead, but it is still possible to kill a vampire; a stake through the heart, or sunlight even, then it's bye- bye batty.

"What about holy water, or a crucifix?"

"Ah, tall tales made up by the church claiming we are demons, or servants of Satan, neither has ever been true. We are conceived, carried, and born into the world the same as all other people. We have as much right to religion and our own beliefs just like anyone else in this world."

"So, without the amulet what happens now?"

"Well without it I will no longer be able to claim my birthright. But first there is something much more important that needs attention." Then he stepped down in the center circle, grabbed my hand and lead me toward the book. "Jezebel are you ready to claim *your* birthright and destiny as the last and only descendant of the clan of Sanballet."

"How do I even know that I am a descendant?"

"Well, we are about to find out!" He said excitingly as he ran behind the podium and then turned to face me. Then he opened the book and began fanning through the pages. They were all blank. "Only a true Sanballet will be able to restore the grimoires power and help locate the Sapphire amulet. Are you sure you are ready to claim the power that you were meant to wield?"

As I stood there in front of the empty book, I thought back to being a little girl and wanting nothing more than a life of magic, adventure, and love. How I would read books just to escape this world hoping to find a place that would satisfy my desire for the extraordinary. Little did I know that what I had been searching for all along was in the world I was so desperate to escape.

"I was born ready!" I said surer than I ever had been. "What do I have to do?"

Then he slammed the book close and looked me in the eye, "All you have to do is touch it and the book will do the reset." Then he quickly ran out of the circle back to the second ring.

I stood just in front of this magnificent book ready to claim what my heart had been telling me I wanted from the moment I was born. My stomach was tied in a knot, as I approached the book a little closer, I began to get nervous. Afraid of what it would mean if the book rejected me, I wanted so badly for this to work. Then I tried to push the thoughts out of my head and focus on the task at hand. I decided that I had to trust in myself and my abilities.

Then just as I approached the book, I placed my right hand firmly onto the leather-bound cover. My heart suddenly sunk into my stomach because nothing happened. With my hand still on the book I began looking around me, thinking that maybe I had missed something, and I wasn't crazy. Searching for any ounce of hope that I could possibly find. Then finally turning to look at Sebastian who was still standing on the second ring off to my left, his arms crossed in front of him. I looked at him as if he knew what was wrong, but he looked just as confused and disappointed as I did.

"Maybe try both hands." He said unsurely with a slight shoulder shrug. So, without hesitation I took my left hand, delicately placing it on the book.

Then suddenly the entire room began to shake, and beneath my feet the stone bricks of the circle I was standing in seemed to wobble. Then out of nowhere a sudden breeze came roaring up, my hair and clothes flying and swirling in the air. Beams of sparkling golden light came shooting up through the cracks in the floor. The light shot all the way up past the second level to the ceiling above. Then what seemed to be a hidden emblem appeared in the bricks beneath me, letting in more light. Then off to my left I could hear Sebastian's jolly laughter as he stood witness to what was happening in the center circle.

Then it all of once seemed to die down, and Sebastian with his continuous laughter began clapping, as he ran into the circle. Then he stood just in front of me, his laughter now gone, and bending down to look me in the eye.

"Are you alright?" He said noticing my blank expression.

"What the heck was that?" I said sternly with my hands still placed firmly on both sides of the book, as if to steady myself.

Then grinning from ear to ear he said, "That was magic. Isn't it marvelous?"

Then removing my hands from the book, I looked at him, suddenly becoming very dizzy. I lost my balance, and began to collapse to the floor, but Sebastian sped behind me and caught me, like we were doing a trust exercise.

"Whoa! How about we take a little break now? Does that sound good?" he asked as he sat me on the step that separated the second level from the center circle.

"What happened?" I asked slightly out of breath.

"Well, the book recognized the magic in your blood, so you then were able to claim your heritage."

"But didn't I already have the ability to use magic without it?"

"Yes, you were born that way, but until now you had no control of the power. It was using you, like a battery, but now it will bend to your will."

"How come I never had the ability to use it before this morning?"

"I would think it is because you had never been with me before, it seems your body suddenly woke the ability from spending time with me."

"I would say that sounds a bit cocky of you, but it also makes sense, considering we do share a soul. So, I will let you get away with it this time." Then he just laughed, climbing back to his feet.

"Are you ready to see if it worked?"

"Yeah." Then I reached out my hand for him to help me to my feet, and we walked back to the book.

Opening it to find beautifully handwritten script, spells, enchantments and even potion recipes. There were even loose papers, clippings, plants, and even small baggies filled with seeds, roots and even what looked like hair, in the book that wasn't there before. Then suddenly as we were flipping through the pages a growling noise seemed to fill the room. We both immediately froze, then it roared again, blushing embarrassed I held my hand over my stomach. I awkwardly smiled as my stomach continued to sound once more.

"Seems like it's time to take a break and grab something to eat." He said in an amused voice.

"Yeah, I suppose it is."

Then we turned to leave the room and as we walked down the hall and around the corner the bookcase seemed to put itself back in its rightful place in the wall. I paused and looked down the hall one more time. I smiled, remembering everything that had been said and that had happened. Knowing that I no longer had to be afraid of feeling like I was crazy, cause it was real. I didn't imagine it at all. I am a powerful witch and I now possessed something utterly amazing. Then I continued walking as I caught up with Sebastian, knowing that the future held something remarkable.

Chapter

XIX

We made our way down the hall, down some stairs and around several corners back tracking to the front of the house. We walked down the same way we had come, walking down the hall I noticed one small difference. Where the giant crystal framed windows were beautifully displayed before were now shielded. The long velvet curtains that were parted before, were now pulled closed.

"You really are a Vampire, aren't you?" I said more to myself than anyone, but still loud enough for him to hear me.

"Yeah, why the doubt all a sudden? After everything that just happened you…?" Then cutting him off I said.

"Not doubting, just noticed the crystal windows are covered. They were open when I arrived."

"Ah, yes the housekeepers draw the drapes at dawn."

"Do they know?"

"No. But I am sure they have their theories about me and my strange ways." He said the last part in a spooky tone. With wide eyes and raised eyebrows like he was telling a ghost story. Wiggling his fingers in the clichéd way that people do when they want to add scary emphasis. Then his expression melted away to a grin as he chuckled in amusement, as if he had told himself a joke. I gave him a nudge as we made our way through the hall, leaving the windows behind us.

"OMG!" I jabbered at him in realization, stopping dead in my tracks.

"What? Is something wrong?" He asked shifting his mood quickly in reaction to my outburst.

Looking him in the eye and with no expression, I said as serious as I could manage. "The façade has finally shattered."

"What are you talking about?" he said genuinely confused.

"You, you are such a dork!" I said through explosive laughter. I was laughing so hard I couldn't breathe and had to hold my stomach because my muscles were getting sore.

"I am not a dork." He said plainly, crossing his arms not amused by my chortling reaction. I couldn't speak because I was still laughing so I nodded instead. A few minutes later I was finally coming down from my high, enough to catch my breath but still giggling a little.

"I am not a dork!" He said again this time more firmly, and then turned and continued walking.

"Hey, wait up." I said running after him. Then standing at his side I continued, "I am sorry I didn't mean to laugh at you, but I couldn't help myself. I have been doubting this entire situation. Not to men I was afraid could never live up to your status because I am a dork too. I don't have any experience with any of this." I said as I gestured to the interior of the mansion.

"I don't think you're a dork, I think you are beautiful." I blushed not quite sure what to say, shocked at the sudden shift the conversation had taken. Trying hard to resist the butterfly feeling in my stomach. Just when I was starting to think that he was more than just a pampered-rich-player.

Then we started walking down the stairs into the front hall. I looked up to look at the beautiful breathtaking chandelier again. Twinkling and sparkling in the light as it hung in its brilliance from the ceiling. I couldn't take my eyes off it, suddenly I knew what it was about the situation that had me second guessing everything.

"This is almost unreal; I am not sure how to feel about it?"

"About what?"

"About everything! My entire life has completely flipped, practically overnight. Two weeks ago, I was a heartbroken-gossip columnist. My biggest concern was letting my roommate make dinner. Now I am an unemployed witch who's inside some amazing guys mansion, that has a chandelier bigger than my bedroom. Oh, and here's another twist he also just so happens to also be a vampire.

And on top of all that, I now know why my entire life I have been lost and felt robbed of my identity, because I am not me! Kind of wish someone had left me a note you know. Dear Jez, Welcome to life it's nice to have you, oh p.s. you are the reincarnation of someone else, so don't fuck it up this time. Good luck!"

Then panting out of breath I looked at him as he stared back at me stunned. He looked at me as if I were a bomb timer that was slowly reaching zero. At first, he didn't say anything, he just stood expressionless leaning away from me. Then after he was sure I wasn't going to completely blow my top he straightened out and said.

"Are you going to be alright?" He said it a little sarcastic but also sincere. He was looking at me like a worried mother whose kids just found out Santa's not real.

"Yeah. I think I'll be fine, it felt good to say it all at once out loud like that. You know put it out into the universe and just own it." Then he nodded, and I could see the worry vanish away.

Then we finally made it to the French doors leading into the dining room. He opened the door for me and gestured with his other hand for me to enter.

Shaking my head, I said, "No I am gonna give Ashton a call really quick. I left suddenly without saying anything to her and I want to be sure she is doing better."

"Okay. Is everything alright?"

"Yeah, everything is great I want to be sure she knows I am okay, she tends to be very overprotective of me." I said smiling, trying hard to convince him that was all it was. He smiled back at me skeptical of my tone but agreed and continue through the door. "I will be right in." I shouted after him as he entered through the doors.

Then turning away, I took out my phone and called Ashton. I waited patiently as the phone rang and the more it rang the more anxious, I became. Then finally the phone went to her voicemail. I listened to her mailbox recording, feeling sort of relieved it wasn't really her. This guilt was eating me alive, and I didn't know if I should even tell Sebastian about it. It was like if I said it out loud it would make me really feel like a monster. Then I heard the beep signaling that I could record my message.

"Hey Ashton, its Jezebel, I wanted to let you know that I'm okay. I also wanted to let you know I am really sorry about what happened earlier. Just know that I have all the answers I need now. I am ready to…" Then the mailbox beeped at me for the second time, signaling that I was out of time.

So, annoyed I hung up the phone and tucked it away in my pocket and began making my way through the French doors. Then my phone vibrated. Standing in the doorway propping it open with my body I took my phone out again. Looking at it hoping it was a text message from Ashton. It was my mother asking me again when a good time would be to come and visit, so as usual I ignored it and put my phone away.

I walked into the kitchen and saw something I wasn't expecting. Not that anyone should ever expect to walk in a kitchen to find someone sucking on a slab of meat, that they held dangling in the air above them. I stopped in my tracks making an involuntary noise at the sight I had walked in on. Oddly enough I think it beat out the sight in the ticket booth from the concert a few weeks ago.

Sebastian realizing, he was no longer alone with his animal flesh. Dropped the meat onto a plate that was sitting on the center island counter behind him. Then quickly grabbing a towel to wipe his face and hands free of any evidence.

"Sorry!" He said obviously a little mortified and startled.

"No, its fine I will learn to get used to it."

"Thanks," he said a little coy, with a hint of shame. Then walking over to where he was, I looked down at the steak that was now bone dry on the plate in front of me. Then I looked up at him and with as much sympathy as I could manage, I said, "Is that really how you live?"

"I am not quite sure what you mean?"

"You suck on pieces of meat?" I said a little grossed out poking at the meat with my finger like it was a science experiment.

"Yeah, why is it gross?"

"Well yeah, but I was mostly referring to how disappointing that must be. Have you ever eaten human food?"

"No, I was born a vampire, so I have always lived off blood, I can eat some meat, but it can't be cooked at all, but for the most part just blood."

"Have you always eaten..." I paused trying hard to get the words out. But distracted by the thoughts of what the answer might be and finally finishing, "animals?"

"No." he said bluntly once again with a hint of shame. "There was once a time when I didn't have to hide my true nature from the world. We, my family and I, would survive off the blood of prisoners locked in the dungeon of the castle where I grew up."

"Wait you grew up in a castle?"

"I say I grew up by draining people and the only part you care about is the castle?"

"I mean it's not like you were going around pillaging and killing people. You killed men who were guilty and were being punished for doing something wrong."

"I don't care, I hated it! I hated it then and I hate it now. I can still hear my father's voice saying I was a disappointment to the clan. The taste of human blood makes a vampire ravenous; they kill and kill until there are whole villages gone. You can taste the fear in their blood, completely rewiring your psyche. Then your whole being is powered only by the urges and desire for human flesh. Until you're so far into the frenzy you've lost yourself to what you are instead of who. This was especially difficult as a child when it is harder to control your urges. I didn't know if I should stay true to myself or my father's wishes. It was torcher!" Then he dropped his head and smashed his fist on the countertop. Clearly angry and disgusted by the thoughts and memories in his head. I didn't know how to react until I saw a single tear roll down his cheek.

"Hey now." I said slowly walking over to him, lifting his head till his eyes met mine, I wiped the tear away with my thumb.

"There is no need for any of that, you're not a monster and you never have to be again." Then I smiled reassuringly until I saw his expression lighten up and he responded.

"I am so glad I can finally talk to you about who I really am, it was so hard having to pretend before."

"I am glad you can too. You never have to hide anything from me. I am a very understanding person, or so I've heard." He said nothing just nodded, reassuring me that he was alright. Then he took a deep breath, turned, and walked over the large stainless-steel refrigerator behind him. As he stood staring at its contents, I did a quick look over of the kitchen.

It is all white, with hints of sky blue and had all silver appliances. In the center of the room is a giant island with a white marble countertop. All the way around the outside of the island are white drawers and cupboards. Then hanging above the island in the center is a pan rack. The refrigerator sat opposite the entry doors to the Kitchen. To the right of the fridge is the double sink which is also stainless-steel. The sink has tall arched faucet, the sink is in the middle of another white marble countertop. Above the sinks are all white cabinets, and next to that are four wall ovens stacked in rows of two. That behind where I was standing (opposite the sink) are swinging doors that lead to a pantry. Then to my left tucked back a little further was a glass top stove, with its own oven. The walls have cute white wallpaper with vertical blue strips. Finally, the floor has white tiles with blue frames, to match the walls. I thought how interesting it was that the inside of Sebastian's house was the opposite of him and the way he dressed.

Currently he was wearing black laced vans, black loose-fitting jeans with a lot of zippers and a tear in his left knee. A black t-shirt that had red lettering across his chest and a picture of some guys on it. But it was so old and faded I couldn't quite make out who they were, but I assumed it was a band. His hair was a little wilder than usual. I stared as the front of his long dark hair brushed his cheek and shaded his eyes, as he bent over into the fridge. Then I began checking out the way his arm flexed, as he gripped the door handle of the freezer door to his left. Then moving my eyes to the right, a little, I caught sight of his nice round buttocks. Staring in awe I became amazed with it perfectly perky shape.

"See something you like?" I turned to face him, and my expression immediately change when his face met mine. He grinned at me and raised his eyebrows and flashed me a cocky sideways grin. I stared at him with a deer in the headlights look, as he batted his eyes at me.

"What?" I finally said bugging my eyes out at him a little nervous knowing I had been caught gawking at him.

Then he chuckled, closed the refrigerator door and he walked back toward me. "Oh nothing, just referring to the drop of drool leaking out of the corner of your mouth as you stare at my ass."

"What!" I said wiping my mouth with my hand and blushing in embarrassment. Then he laughed at me when I noticed my mouth was dry. My face beaming bright red feeling a little horrified because I was definitely caught checking him out.

"I was just teasing. There wasn't any drool, but you are blushing slightly."

"Oh, I'm sorry." I said moving my hand from my mouth to my cheek, feeling them get even warmer.

"It's okay." Then changing the subject, he continued with the matter at hand. "Anyway, there isn't anything here for you to eat unless you like me to cook you a steak?"

I giggled, "Uh no thank you, I guess I can run home and get something there. It is about time I head home anyway." Then I started to make my way toward the door of the kitchen. Trying hard to move passed my moment of humiliation. Shifting through the butterflies that had started to arise before getting caught.

"Let me drive you." He said trailing after me.

"No, that is alright I drove myself."

"I know, we will take your car."

"But then how will you get back?"

"Trust me I will be fine, and home in no time."

"What are you gonna do evaporate and teleport back home with some crazy vampy power?" I asked teasingly with a laugh as I slipped on my coat.

"Something like that, yeah." He responded back.

Then opening the huge front door and stepping outside. I turned to see Sebastian, noticing he was standing off to the side far from the door.

"What are you doing?" I asked confused.

"Just making sure it is safe before exiting." Then realizing that he was referring to the sun, I looked at the surrounding area from my spot on the front stoop. I saw a beautiful cool night lit by the bright moon, it turned the landscape various shades of blue and purple. I smiled as the night breeze washed over my face, blowing loose pieces of my bun and bangs backward.

"Yeah, it's safe." I said in a content comforting voice. Then turned back to see him exiting the doorway and moving passed me down the steps. Heading to the car that was still parked at the very bottom of the walkway. Sebastian being the gentleman that he is, opened the passenger side door for me.

"My lady." He said mocking a stereotypical gentleman's voice.

"Why thank you good sir!" I said in the appropriate lady's voice back as I dangled the keys in my hand in front of him.

"Oh and thank you!" He said in the same voice taking them from me, then I climbed into the car, with him closing the door behind me. He then sped around the car in no time at all and climbed into the driver's seat. Then after making sure, we were both wearing seatbelts and all his mirrors were position we were off.

CHAPTER

XX

Sebastian and I were sitting in the front seats of my car heading down his driveway. I gawked at him as he turned on the main rode from the gate entrance, he had the driver's side window cracked a little. The night air and all its glorious smells leaked into the car as he sped down the road. It also blew his long bangs backward just enough to make his dreamy existence amplify from movie star status to guardian angel. Then acknowledging the eerie silence in the small space, we took up, I decided to strike up a conversation.

"So how do you know how to drive?"

"I'm a vampire not a Neanderthal, I am with the times!"

Then I laughed, "Uh, not if you are still using phrases like 'with the times'. What I meant was, how does someone like you get a license? Do you get weird looks being a grown man walking into the DMV with no driver's license?"

"I have actually been alive longer than the existence of the automobile. So, it wasn't weird because I was getting one the same time as everyone else."

"Wow! Really? How old are you?"

"Nope! Sorry if I told you that, it might completely ruin our relationship."

"Really, after everything you have told me? You think a measly little number is gonna be the deal breaker?" I said teasingly, trying to convince him to tell.

"That is just the thing, it is not a measly little number." He said firmly, as if nothing I could say would make him crack.

"Pwease Sebastian!" I said sweetly batting my eyes at him, like a child begging for candy. Followed by whiny dog sounds, and the classic puppy dog face, curling my bottom lip and making sad eyes at him.

"Okay! Fine, but I warned you. I was born on a Thursday evening on October 23rd, 1687. You can do the math yourself." He said playfully, taunting me with the information.

So, I took out my phone and pulled up my calculator app. I started typing in the numbers, 2018 minus 1687, shocked at the results. I didn't even know how to respond, I knew when I was typing in the numbers it would be big, but not that big.

"You're 330 years old!" I blurted in astonishment. "That is amazing! You have been around for so long. How do you possibly look so young?"

"Okay, ouch! First of all, that hurt, but I am going to go ahead and file that in the compliment pile! Second of all, I am actually still fairly young for a vampire, and will never look older than I do now. Vampires are immortal, that means we don't age or die unless killed, like lobsters or jellyfish."

"You just compared yourself to a jellyfish." I said not quite sure what point I was trying to make, then I continued with the conversation. "That is actually really cool. Why did you not want to tell me how old you are?"

"I figured it might be a little weird for you to know how old I actually am. At least if you didn't know, you could pretend I am not centuries older than you."

"I actually don't mind; I mean it might be a different story if you looked your age. Since you don't my mind I can still pretend."

Then I turned away from him as we finally entered the out skirts of the city. I looked at all the lights and felt the vibe shift as he rolled up his window, and we were now passing cars not trees. I sighed at the thought of what would be awaiting me back home.

"What is the matter?" He asked sincerely.

"Well, I got fired from my job at the magazine, I didn't want to work there anymore anyway, but I still need a job. Then something happened with Ashton, when I got home, that I hope doesn't scare her away from me forever. I am not looking forward to jumping right back into my life after the way I left it, but I know I have to." Then sagging my head and frowning I tried to overcome it.

"I am sorry to hear about your job, but if it's any consolation I am here for you whenever you need me. If you need a place to run away to and shut out the world. I know a place with lots of space and huge curtains that block out every square inch of the world behind them."

"Thanks." I said smiling coyly at him as I lifted my head back up.

"What happened with Ashton exactly? Maybe I can help."

"Well, it is kind of embarrassing, and I am afraid of what it will mean if I say it out loud."

"It will mean you are brave enough to acknowledge the truth and strong enough to overcome it." I sat amazed, not about how Sebastian knew exactly the right thing to say, but how right he was. It was what I needed to hear to boost me back up. This is who I am now and if I expect others to except it then I will need to except it first.

"Thank you, Sebastian. That really helped." Then smiling at each other as the car turned the corner. Pulling into the parking garage of my apartment building. We parked in my personal space, and he turn off the engine. Then still sitting in the car he asked, "So you gonna tell me what happened?"

Then in a soft, humiliated tone I told him what I did, "I accidentally attacked her with my magic. I was freaking out because of something else that happened at work when I got fired. I was sitting on the floor when she came up behind me and startled me. When I turned to face her, I somehow sent her flying into a wall filled with pictures. She got hurt and is not speaking to me right now."

"Oh, why didn't you tell me before? Is she going to be alright? How bad was she hurt? What does she think happened?" He said quickly, rambling off everything that popped into his head at one time.

"Well like I said I was afraid of being a monster, and yes she'll be fine she got a little shard of glass in her hand. To be honest I don't know what she thinks. I haven't spoken to her since it happened."

"Well, I am sure that she loves you enough to understand, and maybe it is good that you left when you did. It gave her time to process everything alone, and now that your back she might be ready to talk."

"I hope you are right." I said taking a deep breath, then stepping out of the car.

We both started to walk toward the elevator when he changed the subject. "So, considering the circumstances and seeing as you don't have a job, well at least until you get a new one, it would be wise to take this time for you to learn to master your magic. So, you don't accidently attack other people with your gifts. Don't forget I know firsthand how lethal you can be without it, you're lucky I am indestructible. But I don't want someone whose not to find out how dangerous you can be."

Then I giggled at his attempt to lighten the subject and said, "Your right."

"So, how about you come back to the house tomorrow evening, and I will teach you some of the basics."

"That sounds great!" I said smiling at him as I hit the elevator call button. Then we rode the elevator all the way up in silence, grinning at each other. Then we made our way down the hall and to the front door of my loft. I placed my hand on the door ready to enter when I turned to him abruptly. "You know it is best I go in alone, considering. I would love to invite you in, but I think until things with Ashton are all cleared it is better I go in alone. But thank you so much for everything, I look forward to our future journeys together."

"I understand, I am glad you came to me. And I am even more glad you know the truth now. I hope all goes well with your friend. I hope to meet her again one day."

"Yeah, that would be fun." I said awkwardly, not quite sure how to comfortably end the conversation.

"Well, goodnight Jezebel." He finally said, breaking into the awkwardness. Then he grabbed my hand and kissed it with a bow and walked back toward the elevator.

I entered the loft and noticed it was quiet, I assumed Ashton had gone to bed. I put down my bag and hung my coat. When I was taking off my shoes I got hit in the face with a throw pillow. I looked up to find Ashton standing on the other side of the coach. She was holding another pillow as a shield or if need be, more ammo. Crouched into a defensive stance she stood solid, staring at me.

"What the heck did you do that for?" I said in annoyed confusion.

"Stay back!" She blurted back at me. Then realizing I wasn't walking into a welcome home party, or even hug I turned up my defensive.

"Hey, Ashton I am not going to hurt you. I said I was sorry, I feel terrible. I was as scared as you are now. I didn't know what was happening to me." She said nothing just stood in the same stiffened stance, so I tried to approach her. Taking a step toward her I was hit once again in the face with a throw pillow.

"You know that's not why they call them throw pillows. Right?" I said trying to break throw the tension. Then trying once more to approach her. I didn't get more than halfway there before she armed herself with more fluffy ammo.

"Ashton, put the pillow down." I said firmly. Stopping in my tracks putting my hands out in front of me as my only protection from her cotton filled blasts. We stood for a moment staring at each other trying to decide who would make the next move. Being bold I started making my way toward her again. This time I was able to dodge her attack after she first yelled, "Stay away from me!" Then running away from me toward her bedroom.

"Ashton, I just want to talk. I can explain everything now!" I said chasing her across the loft.

"No! Stay back you monster!" she said before slamming her bedroom door in my face. I stood outside the closed door petrified after being hit with the worst thing she'd throw at me. Then I felt the tear rolling down my cheek, it was cold and was moving at a snail's pace, I wiped it was with my hand. Not quite sure what to do next, I dropped to the floor in front of her closed bedroom door.

"Ashton," I sobbed softly, "I am sorry." I didn't hear a response, or even any moved from the other side. So, I pulled my legs to my chest and buried my face in my knees. Wrapping my head with my arms and sobbing. Realizing that not only did my identity change, but everything that I had with my old self, left with it.

CHAPTER

XXI

I sat on the floor outside Ashton's bedroom crying into my lap for about ten minutes. Then I finally heard some movement inside her room. I heard soft slow footstep, then I heard her turning the doorknob slowly and the door creak open. She crouched down onto the floor in front of me, and I felt her run her hand down the side of my head, petting my hair gently.

"Hey, I am sorry. I shouldn't have called you a monster, I love you no matter who you are." She said softly, still stroking my hair.

"Thanks, I love you too. I don't' know what I would do if you rejected me, for any reason." I said slowly brightening up, relieved she was talking to me again.

"So, you told me you had all the answers now, I am ready to hear them."

"Okay, but can we get off the floor first. Also, I am like hungry."

"Yeah, that sound good, and I have some left-over Chinese in the fridge. Don't worry I didn't cook it myself." She said smiling, making me giggle.

Then getting up from the floor I wiped my tears with my sleeves and we walked into the kitchen. I opened the fridge and pulled out the left-over Chinese food boxes. Ashton helped separated them onto two plates and pop each one into the microwave. Then as I came to join Ashton at the kitchen table, we ate silently at first. Hearing nothing but our forks clinking against our plates, until finally she spoke up.

"So, where did you go after, you know?"

"I went to see Sebastian actually. Do you remember exactly what happened before I left?"

"Not sure, I remember you sitting on the floor crying. Then I remember banging into something and a huge crashing noise. Next thing I know I am sitting on the floor surrounded my broken glass and my hand is stinging. The rest I kind of tuned out. Then I am waking up in my bedroom confused and unsure of how I even got there, and you were gone. I searched the house and even called the magazine. When I received your phone call is when I remembered you are the one who through me across the room. I am still not sure how you did it. I know that whatever it was I'm probably not going to like it."

"Yeah, for the most part you have all the important details. Now, I am going to tell you how I throw you, and I am warning you that it is a lot to take in, but I promise it is nothing to be afraid of." I said waiting for her response, but she was just nodding in understanding. "I am not like other people. I am something that other people believe isn't even real. I am a witch." I said reluctantly, hoping that once the words left my lips and entered her ears that she would not scream or panic.

"That is all?" she said nonchalantly. Please by her response I took a deep breath of relief.

"What do you mean that is all? That seems like some pretty loaded new."

"Well yeah it is pretty loaded, but it also makes sense. I was sitting around trying to figure out how you did what you did. I had already considered that possibility. Not in the logical way people consider things. But when they run out of logical explanations and have to resort to possible supernatural explanation."

"Well, I am relieved you took it so well, I am still trying to figure it out for myself."

"How do you know for sure?"

"Well for starters I sent my desk at work on fire when Miranda approached me about being let go."

"Oh crap! You did what? What happened?"

"Don't worry about it, I didn't want to work there anyway."

"No, I meant with the fire."

"Oh, I am not really sure. I left as soon as the emergency sprinklers when off." She said nothing, she sat staring at me for a short while, and then I spoke up again. "I am sure everything is fine, it was only a small fire and the fire department is notified when the sprinklers go off."

"Well I hope everyone is okay, but yeah I guess that would confirm the ability of magic."

"That and Sebastian told me what I am when I went to go see him. That is another thing I should tell you, Sebastian is not like other people either."

"Oh, so he is a witch too?"

"No, he is, well he's a..." I struggled to get the word out finding it even more difficult to admit than my being a witch, "he is a vampire."

"Now you're pulling my leg. Right?"

"I'm sorry, no. He is a real vampire, but don't worry he will never hurt me or anyone for that matter."

"How do you know that!"

"Ashton, I walked in on him draining a sirloin steak bone dry. He says he doesn't like eating people, and he was very torn up about it too." Once more she didn't say anything she collected our now empty plates and took then to the sink. I got up from the table and walked to the counter behind where she was standing. "Is everything alright?"

"Yes, everything is fine, I don't know what to say I have never had a literal conversation about these kinds of things. So, finding something real to say is hard."

"I understand, well we don't have to talk about it anymore then. I have something else to talk about that I'm sure is going to pep you right back up."

"I will be the judge of that." She said in a sassy, teasing tone.

"Seeing as I don't have a job anymore, I want to audition for that part you've been telling me about." Then she squealed with excitement, running around the counter to hug me. She stood squeezing me so hard I could hardly breathe, saying the best I could without oxygen, "I figure why not give it a shot."

"I am so excited!" she screamed excitingly still squeezing me. Then letting me go in a worried serious tone she asked. "Your not gonna be going around attacking people putting hexes on them or anything like that right?"

"No." I said plainly, confused at her random question.

"Okay then your hired, I mean of course you still have to audition, theatre policy, but your hired." She said shaking me. Then turning and heading back toward her room she said. "I am going to run and grab the script and we can run a few lines before your audition tomorrow."

Then as she disappeared, and I stood alone in the kitchen. Feeling my nerves already starting to tighten up already I whispered to myself. "Tomorrow?" Then I swallowed hard petrified of what might happen. I took a deep breath and wondered what I had gotten myself into.

CHAPTER

XXII

Ashton and I had been up almost all night going over the lines for the fairy part, and I didn't realize how big of a role it was. We spent a lot of time with her telling me to make the part my own. But ultimately always ended up with Ashton explaining the vison she had of the character. Which made me feel even more nervous as I realized my bestie/roommate was also now my boss.

We headed to the theatre early that morning and she showed me around the backstage area. Once the entire cast had shown up for rehearsal; she had me standing center stage reading the scene we had practiced.

"You are not welcome here" I said in the best scary voice I could manage.

"Who are you?" Ashton said in her best brave dude's voice, reading the lines of the male lead from the audience seats.

"I am the black fairy, and I warn you if you trespass on this property you shall be forever cursed!" I said doing my best to make a fairy seem threatening.

"You are no threat to us! Now be gone you overgrown fly!" Ashton said still doing her male voice. Then continuing reading the supporting male leads line, changing her voice to seem more frigid. "Yeah, what he said."

"I will not be intimidated by such…" Then Ashton cut me off before the end of the line.

"Jezebel, I need you to read this line with more power. Let them know that you will not be crossed, or else. Okay?"

"Okay." Then continuing my lines, I said like I was this all-powerful black fairy, giving into the illusion. "I will NOT be intimated by such filthy creatures. I am the Black Fairy of Skye and I have never been defeated by a mere mortal."

"Well then today will be my lucky day. I intend separate your head from your body and carry it to my castle to display with my other trophies." She said in the male leads voice again, as threating and macho as she could.

"Foolish human, you have no power here!"

"That was great!" Ashton said in her normal voice, "You will be perfect for this role."

"I did it! I got the job?" I asked surprised.

"Yes! I am going to send you with Linda." She said pointing to an older lady of to my left, who was waving to me. "She is going to go over some costume things with you and play with some make-up looks. Then after lunch you're going to join in with the rest of the cast so study up."

"You got it boss!" I said full of excitement, which surprised me considering I was so nervous. Ashton flashing me one last smile, then turning to her assistant who had brought her a fresh mug of coffee.

Then I pivoted and walked over to Linda who was a shorter lady, with pale skin, curly orange hair and glasses. She had a very kind, round face and was still smiling at me as I approached her. Her glasses were lime green and covering most of her face. She wore a simple look; denim jeans and white shirt with a vampire bat on the front and the phrase 'what is your type?' printed across her chest in red lettering. Which was funny to me considering I now knew a real vampire, and would never think of Halloween the same again.

"Hi, my name is Jezebel it's nice to meet you Linda." I said as I reached my hand out to shake hers. She grabbed it with stone cold hands, and a firmer grip than I had expected from a small elderly woman.

"Hello, congratulation!" she said with a bit of an accent, but I couldn't quite place it. "Let's go ahead and start with makeup. I want to get a feel for your features."

"Okay, sounds good." Then we headed back stage, I could hear the other actors getting into position for a scene behind me as we walked away. I felt a sudden adrenaline rush, something I hadn't felt for a job in a long time. Even as a waitress I felt a sort of exciting rush. I had forgotten how great it felt until now.

We walked backstage and down a hallway. The back stage is shaped like a "H". There are two main hallways on the sides with dressing room on the outer walls. Then there's one main hall connecting them together right behind the back wall of the stage. Below the "H" line was the stage, above it you had the props room in the left hall and costumes and make-up on the right. We entered the make-up room which had a cute decorative plaque on the door that said, '*disguise design*.' I giggled at the sign, because it has a female vampire putting on make-up in a mirror. Considering she had no reflection, she looked quite annoyed.

In the far-right corner of the room there is a cute little dressing room area. Exactly like you would see in a department store. The rooms are facing outward along the right wall toward the left side of the room. There are five stalls and instead of doors they have curtains. There was a separation wall in front of the stalls, making a little hall for the dressing stalls.

Then to the left of the stalls there is a huge closet area with a rack full of wardrobe selection of all sorts. Then above the rack is a shelf full of prosthetics, body paints, and costume tools. Then on the wall to the right is a floor to ceiling shelf of male shoes. Then on the opposite side, the separation wall, is another floor to ceiling shelf filled with women's shoes.

Then there is a desk and a small table to the left of me. To my right is a giant mirror and a long counter. Covering the counter top is lots of tubs of makeup, cups full of brushes, sponges and cotton balls. Finally there is four salon chairs, spread evenly in front of the counter.

Linda had approached the counter and spun the chair around for me to take a seat, smiling at me excitingly. I took my seat and she spun me around to face the mirror. then peeking out from behind the chair she asked my reflection. "Would you like something to snack on while we are playing around with some looks."

Shocked by the offer I kindly declined, "No thank you, maybe later though."

"Okay, well first off I need to know if you have any skin conditions or allergies to any products. Most of what I use is organic but for the prosthetics I use and non-organic material. It tends to leave a skin reaction on some people with softer skin."

"No, I don't have any allergies. But I also have never worn prosthetic, so we will find out how they make me feel."

"Sounds guid." And it was in that small phase when I realized she had a Scottish accent. "Okay, well since I already have yur costume designed and ready to go. I wunt to play with ye face and see whut looks best based on yur personal features. So, ye are the black fairy, yes?" I knew it wasn't an actual question, but I found myself nodding anyway. "So ye makeup wi' consist of dark colors, loch black, gray, maybe sae dark tones like broon, purple an' blue. We of course are gonnae lighten ye base and give ye a bit of a blue tint."

Then grabbing some light gray, white and baby blue face paint. Mixed them together in a bowl to make kind of a blue color that was still on the white side. Then with a make-up sponge she started applying the paint to my face as a foundation.

"Ye hae beautiful skin, just gorgeous." She said as she coated my entire face in paint.

"Thank you." I said shyly, not sure how else to respond.

Then she played around with some different eyeliner wings, shapes and even tried a design on the side of my face. She tried various combinations of make-up colors. Making numerous kinds of Smokey eyes, ombres or even cut crease looks on my eyes with each combo. Then she played around with various lipstick colors and styles. She did lots of different effects with shading and contouring. And in the process getting glitter everywhere. She even did some ear point extensions with prosthetics.

Then we made a final decision on a look and started playing with the costume. She pulled out a large wardrobe bag and unzipped it. It had the most perfect fairy costume I had ever seen inside it. She helped me into it, and it fit like a glove. Aside from the shoulder which were a little too big and kept sliding down my left arm.

Then we went through several different shoes deciding on some flat heeled boots. They have an up curved rim around my knee, meaning they rose to a peak in the front. Then when she was putting in the pins to fix the shoulders Ashton's assist came to the door and announced lunch.

"Thank ye sweetheart, we will be right there." Linda said in her sweet soft voice, then she turned back to me and finished pinning the costume.

"All done, now fur th' bosses' approval." She said smiling and then making her way toward the door.

We walk back to the stage, and I tried extremely hard not to stab my shoulders with a needle as I moved. We walked onto the stage and found Ashton talking to some guy on stage.

"Whut ye think?" Linda blurted, interrupting Ashton's conversation with the man.

"Oh my, that is perfect, well done Linda!" Ashton said then excused the man for lunch and continued. "Do you know what you're going to do with her hair. She has so much of it you could probably do anything you wanted."

"I figure nah to do too much wi' it, I don't want it to distract from the makeup."

"I like that actually, your right. This masterpiece you've created deserves all the attention. What do you think of it Jez?"

"I think it is absolutely amazing, she is so talented and brilliant." I said blushing with a bit of a smile, feeling the warmth even through the five pounds of makeup on my face.

"That she is, so go ahead and take your photos Linda, then you and Jez can come join everyone else for lunch." Linda nodding and shooed me off the stage. We head back to the 'disguise design' room. Linda took 360-degree photo of every inch of my face and the detailing of my eye makeup. Then she took some full body photos. Then I headed to the closet area to change back into my clothes.

"Ye going on without me, I hae to send in these photos to be printed an added to the book." She said sitting at the desk uploading the photos to the computer.

"The book?" I said a little worried about what she could be referring to.

"Ah, yes the book." She said as she pulled out a thick binder from the shelf above the desk, with the play title written on the front. "It has aw the costumes and makeup designs for each character. Helps auld ladies, like me, remember whit they are." Then she let out a soft laugh that was as sweet as her voice.

"Okay, well I will see later then. It was lovey to meet you."

"Sam to ye, lassie."

Then I waved goodbye and headed back to the stage, and Ashton was waiting for me. Then she walked with me to the lounge, which was a room back toward the front entrance of the theatre. We talked about things she had recently added to the play. She was telling me about the harness I was going to have to wear to make me fly. Not sure if I am allowed to give my input yet, so I just nodded in agreeance.

CHAPTER

XXIII

Then we made it to the lounge, sub sandwiches had been laid out on a giant tray. Also set out next to the tray were mini bags of chips and a veggie platter. And to drink were some boxes of canned soda on the table along with a case of water.

"Help yourself." Said Ashton as she picks up a plate and started in on the table of food. Still a little out of my comfort zone I picked up a plate and started grabbing some food slowly. Then Ashton and I took some seats at a table in the middle of the room.

"So, I have been meaning to ask you something that I thought about earlier this morning but forgot."

"Yeah, ask me anything."

"Are you and Sebastian a thing, like are you official."

"Um, you know we haven't really discussed and right now I'm defiantly getting more of a friend vibe. Like we flirt but were not an item yet, at least I don't think so. Why?"

"Well, I started talking to this new guy, but I don't want it to make seem like he has a chance at something solid. So, I was hoping we could double. You know to make it a little less intimate between me and this guy.

"Um, well I plan on going to see Sebastian tonight, I can ask. Even if we are going as friends, I'm sure he would like another chance at a date with me."

"Oh, so your gonna ask him on date."

"No! I mean, well maybe." Then I blushed and bite my bottom lip.

"How did you react when you found out that he was a..." Then she paused to look and see if anyone was around, and then whispered, "a vampire."

"Well considering I had already figured it out, all he pretty had to do was confess, so it wasn't that crazy. But learning about him and his experiences is fascinating, and I love the way he makes me feel so alive. You know he is 330 years old, just image all the things he knows."

"Damn! He is that old, that's kind of gross."

"Oh shut-up you didn't even notice and would have never know had I not said anything." I said laughing.

"True." She said still disgusted by the thought but also relieved.

Then we finished our sandwiches within a few hours and headed back for rehearsals. It was a great rehearsal, and I was picking up the lines fairly quickly. It was some of the stage directions however that had me thrown. When I wasn't onstage, I was filling out employment papers for the theater. After another three- or four-hours Ashton announced that that was a wrap for the day and will would pick right wear we left off tomorrow.

And I suddenly felt sad knowing it was already time to go home. But also excited because that meant I go to have my first magic lesson and I go to see Sebastian. Ashton and I were the last out of the theater and she locked up. We jumped into her metallic lime green convertible and headed home. The entire way home, I was making notes on the sides of my script. Drawing out the stage directions, hoping it would help me practice the entire way home.

Then after getting home, I switch directly to my car, waved goodbye to Ashton and headed for the mansion. I drove there in what seemed like no time at all and climbed up the front steps and before I was about to know the door swung open. Sebastian was standing bright eyed on the other side.

"You came!" he said excitingly.

"Yes, I said I would didn't I. So, here I am."

"Great, come in." he said stepping aside.

Entering the house, I looked around still not fully prepared for the view that was just in the entrance of the house. Then we started to make our way toward the bookcase and talking the entire way.

"So, I felt bad about last night, so I had Jasper run out and buy some food for you."

"Sebastian, that is so thoughtful, but also not necessary you don't have to feel bad. I was perfectly happy running home."

"I know, but I'd like to accommodate you how ever I need to, considering you might be here often."

"I suppose you have point. Thank you."

"My pleasure. So how did the reunion with your roommate go."

"Ok, well she freaked out a little, but eventually we found our way back. I also told her about you being a vampire. I can do that right?"

"Yeah, it's okay, not like you can un-tell her anyway. But I don't mind as long as you trust her, I will trust her. You trust her, right?"

"Yeah, with my life." I said with a bit of a giggle.

"Okay. Jezebel what is this on your face?" he said wiping something white from my forehead.

"Oh, that's costume paint. Ashton directs at a theater downtown and since I didn't have a job, I finally took up her offer to be in the play. They had me in make-up almost all morning, it was fun, and I met the sweetest lady."

"Oh well congratulation. Your still gonna be able to come over for lessons, right?"

"Of course, I can defiantly do both. It does help that your day start when mine is just about to end."

"Alright, but if you start to feel overwhelmed or even tired let me know and we will take a break. You're welcome to have your own room here. I will have one of my housekeeper's make-up a room for you so that you don't have to drive home if you get to tired. Magic tends to suck a lot of energy, especially if you're a beginner."

"Again, so sweet thank you, you don't have to..."

"No, I want to." He said kindhearted but firm.

"Okay." Then we smiled adoringly like we normally tended to do. I had noticed it was starting to become a habit, but I didn't mind.

Then we made it to the bookshelf, and he pulled out the book and reached back to open the entrance. The book sunk into the wall and to the side revealing the hidden chamber. Walking inside I looked around in awe once more at the newly revealed room. Looking up at the incredibly high ceiling and all the amazing things on the many shelves.

"I am never gonna get used to this."

"You say that now, but just wait eventually you will."

"I hope not, this place is amazing."

"If you think that is amazing just wait till you actually master some of it."

I walked along the outside ring, looking over some of the bottle and tools on the shelves. Then making my way into the center circle I lightly stroked the leather cover of the grimoire. Then turning to Sebastian who was stepping up beside me I said, "Okay chief, where do we begin?"

"First of all, don't call me chief," he said bluntly.

"Got'cha." I said a little timid.

"Second of all the first key to learning magic is to be able to conjure your magic. So, make a flame, move something, anything. Find what it take for you to be able to call forth your magical energy."

I put out my hand and making a fist I did a quick opening motion with my hand, flicking my fingers apart and snapping my wrist. Nothing happened, so I tried it again, and then again and many times. Until finally I looked at Sebastian, wondering if I was doing something wrong.

"Don't' give up! Keep trying! You'll get it eventually." he said encouragingly.

So, I thought back to Miranda and the way she made me angry, or even when I attacked Ashton how I was feeling then too. Focusing on how I did it then. Then, I closed my eyes and took a deep breath, and did it the motion again. This time when I opened my eyes, I saw the most vibrant orange flame in the palm of my hand.

"Well done, now remember your tick because you will need to master it if you going to master magic. Now put it out."

"What?"

"Put it out. You conjured it does not hinder the flame."

Taking another deep breath, I focused. With the turn of my palm downward and closing my hand back into a fist the flame vanished.

"Very good, now do it again." He said grin at me with a sideways smirk and sparkling amber eyes. I grunted and gave him an annoyed glare, then focused again on the flame. Over and over again I made fire and disenchanted it. I did it about twenty times before I finally had enough.

"You were right, I am exhausted, and I haven't even moved from this spot."

"We can take a break, come sit." Then we sat on the step of the stone floor, eat this it will help." He said handing me a little red ball.

"What is it?" I said taking the little red pill from him.

"Candy."

"Oh." Then putting the ball in my mouth, I realized it was a miniature cinnamon flavored jawbreaker. I sucked on the jawbreaker for a few seconds until it completely dissolved. "Thank you. What was that for?"

"That was a blood pill, I just told you it was candy so you would take it."

"Ew, gross!" I exclaim, wishing I hadn't already ingested the pill.

"Relax. It is infused with the magical blood of your family and will help you replenish your strength. It tasted like cinnamon did it not?"

"I mean yes it did, but just the thought of swallowing blood is just so…" Then before I could finish my sentence, I realized how insensitive I was being by the discouraged look on Sebastian's face. "Oh, Sebastian I am so sorry, I didn't mean to…"

"No, that is quite alright. You only just found out, and it takes more than that to upset me." Then there was a brief awkward silence and then I remember I was supposed to ask him something.

"So, I have something important I would like to discuss." I said still kind of coy, trying to break the silence gentle.

"Go on." He said clearly intrigued, and relieved of the subject change.

"What are we?" I inquired firm but lightly trying not to seem to demanding.

"Come again?" He stated confused by my question.

"What is out relationship status? Are we officially together, or are we just friends?"

"Well, I'd like a do-over on our date before I can officially earn the title of being your man."

"That is actually kind of perfect of my next question. Would you like to go on a double date with me? Ashton wants to date this guy but doesn't want to go alone. Will you join us?"

"Not normal my style, but I'll give it a shot. If it's important to you."

"Thank you, and this will give you the opportunity to meet her again. She is like my sister, so it is of extreme importance that you meet her."

"Just let me know the details and I will try to make it on time."

"I will make sure you can." I said nudging him just a little. He didn't say anything he just smile that charming smile of his, and if he wasn't so pale, I would have sworn I saw him blushing as well.

"Ready to do some more, or we done for the day." He questioned me changing the subject once more.

"No, more!" I announced full of energy again.

"Alright I like that attitude," he said standing up offering me his hand. Then we approach the spell book, and he stood on the other side of the stand. "Okay, so now you need to know the different between enchantments, charms and spells. Enchantments are things that affect your abilities for a short period of time depending on your magical strength. So, the better you get with magic the longer your enchantments will last. Charms affect the mind or emotions, nontangible things. They can be either long term or short depend on the purpose. Then you have your Spells and Incantations; Incantations are a serious of spoken words that have a long term or permeant effect on something or someone. Spells don't even need words most times, as you now know. The creating of the flame or the manipulation of objects is how you use a spell. You don't really have say anything aloud for the magic to happen. Make sense?"

"Yes. So how do I know which one which is?"

"Well enchantments tend to be only one or two words, Charms are a short phrase of words, and Incantations are normal a long series of words, or rhymes. And Spells you've pretty already mastered, you just need to learn your command for the magical energy to enact your spell."

"Okay that's easy enough to remember, I guess. So, what's next?"

"You are going to master some more basic level spells, move that chair with your mind." He said pointing at an old wooden chair that sat against the wall off to my right. We continued with me magic lessons for hours, and it wasn't until later that Sebastian finally called it a night. "You must be tired, that is enough for today. Why don't you come see your new room, and rest?"

"My new room! You already have it ready?"

"The truth is I always had it ready. I only wanted to make you think that I was still working on it, so you didn't back out. But there is no turning back now so come see."

Leaving the room, we headed down the hallway and I sudden felt at peace for the first time in weeks. My life for the first time felt right, like everything was perfect just the way it was, and I never wanted it to change. I looked at Sebastian, who was standing at my side leading the way down the hall. I smiled as I suddenly felt a warm feeling in my chest. That was the moment, the moment I knew I was falling in love with him.

Chapter

XXIV

He lead me into the east wing of the mansion, down a long wide hallway. Then he turned into a doorway that was sunken in from the hall. He opened a huge beige colored set of French doors with silver metal accents. As the doors opened, I couldn't believe my eyes. Every room in this house seems to take my breath away and this one was no different.

Right in front of me in the center of the room, against the far wall, is a beautiful canopy bed with sheer white curtains hanging loosely by each of the four-corner posts. Then on either side of the bed is a window with matching curtains, to the ones flowing from the bed. Then between the windows and the bed are two small spaces, occupied on both side by matching glass top nightstands. The bedding and wallpaper are a similar shade of plum purple. At the bottom of the bed is a white bench, upholstered with a crème-colored fabric. There are purple, white, crème and silver throw pillows on the bed and the bench.

To the left of me there is a beautiful white vanity, with silver accents and handles, similar to the ones on the door. Then laid out perfectly on the top the vanity from left to right is a hand mirror, brush and then a comb. White porcelain bottles line the vanity top along the bottom of the mirror and a cup full of different sized makeup brushes. Then a small table on both sides of the vanity with a beautiful crystal lamps on both.

On the other side of the room standing erect is a white wardrobe with double doors. The wardrobe has a column of five drawers on the right side and a small cupboard above the drawers. Next to that is a silver shoe rack, which is currently empty. Then just to the left of the wardrobe is a door, that matched the entrance doors. Then decorating the walls are beautiful canvas paintings, that must have been centuries old.

Walking inside the room I sat on the bench at the foot of the bed. Looking up to see a beautiful chandelier hanging from the incredibly high ceiling. It is not even close to the size of the one in the main hall, but it was just as beautiful. Lastly the ceiling is covered in very decretive calligraphy patters and stunning crown molding. I didn't know what to think of the room as a whole, it has so many gorgeous pieces. Every day I think I have him all figured out and then Sebastian throws another curve ball at me.

"This is all for me?" I remarked still a little in shock.

"Yes, this will be your room when you stay here. Feel free to make yourself as comfortable as you'd like."

"Thank you!" I belted with ecstasy throwing myself at him and wrapping him in a hug. A hug that clearly caught him off guard because he stood awkwardly in my arms the entire time. I let him go and said. "I'm sorry I didn't know how else to say thank you for your hospitality. You have been so sweet to me, and I haven't done anything to deserve it."

"Just your presence alone will suffice." He responded pleasantly with a smile.

"See there you go again being sweet." I said as I sat down on the bench at eh foot of the bed blushing, he smiled at me and changed the subject.

"Well, I suppose I will let you get some sleep. I bet you are exhausted after the long day you've had. If you should need anything pull this rope." He said gesturing to a rope that was hanging beside the door, "One of my servants will come to your aide. Also, if that is too much for you, my room is just down the hall and to the right." I nodded in responds to his instructions signifying that I understood. "Goodnight Jezebel." He said before leaving the room closing the door behind him.

I sat on the bench for a few minutes after he'd left. Then I got up and took off my shoes and blouse, so that I was only wearing my jeans and tank top. I walked over to the wardrobe, feeling the cold tile floor through my socks the entire way. Grabbing both the door handles and swung the doors open. Inside the wardrobe were beautiful evening gowns in various colors and styles. I ran my fingers along the dresses, feeling the different fabrics and patterns. Then I closed the doors and began rummaging through the drawers. There were panty hose, nylon socks, a couple corsets, a few bras, and some regular socks in the first couple drawers. Then I found what I was looking for, a draw full of nightgowns on the left and pajama sets on the right. I pulled out a set of pajamas and carried them over to the right side of the bed.

I slipped out of my jeans and tank, and before unstrapping my bra I looked around the giant room. The room still unfamiliar to me, to be sure I was alone. Then folding up my clothes I placed them on the bench at the foot of the bed next to my bag. I slipped on the black pair of pajama shorts decorated with multicolored stars and matching black tank top with a crescent moon on it surround by bigger multicolored stars. Then turning around to the mystery door that sat next to the wardrobe, I approached it slowly.

Reaching for the silver handle and felt the cold metal against my palm, making me gasp a little. Then I turned the knob unsure of what to expect on the other side. I stood with the door handle turned for a moment, mentally preparing myself for what it could be. Then all at once swung the door open as I stepped inside only to find more of what this house had to offer.

Inside was a beautiful white, creme and plum purple bathroom matching the bed chamber perfectly. To my immediate right a long white counter with a single sink in the middle. Two cupboards below the sink and drawers on both sides of the cupboards. Then along the wall above the counter is a huge mirror lined with lights.

Then in front of me is the porcelain toilet, next to that is a medium sized chamber shower. The shower has a glass sliding door, with a crème-colored towel handing outside the entrance. Then to the right of that tucked back a little past the sink counter is a huge bathtub, big enough for two people. Plum colored rugs on the floor at the foot of the toilet, shower, and tub, and extra-long one in front of the counter.

After I had finished using the facilities and brushing my teeth, with the brush and paste that was already set out for me on the counter. I started staring at my reflection in the mirror, noticing how the person I used to see in the mirror was gone. Along with my new identity and magic abilities I now saw a different person in the mirror. I don't know if it was because I now know that I used to be someone else entirely. Or because my life had changed so drastically in the past few weeks that I felt different about my appearance.

Then wondered about Brigitta, I had been so caught in the details of Sebastian and learning magic and my new job that I didn't even contemplate on her. I kind of excepted the new information and moved on. Now that am I am thinking about her, I can't help but wonder how much like her I am. Am I even allowed to know about her? Did her getting recycle affect me in anyway? Sighing at the many questions I now had, I left the bathroom, closing the door behind me.

I walked to the vanity, taking down my long dark hair and brushing it with the brush laying on the vanity top. Then I finally crawled into bed, after first unburying it from the thousands of throw pillows. As I wedged myself under the thick fluffy plum colored comforter and sheet. I made an involuntary moaning sound at how comfortable the bed was. I don't know if it was the bed or because I was so dang tired, but I seemed melt into it. Fusing together with it and drifting off into a restful sleep. Feeling so blessed and lucky to be me, having such wonder in my life. For the first time I felt like everything was exactly the way it was supposed to be.

Chapter

XXV

The next morning, I woke to my phone alarm going off on the nightstand next to the bed. I reached to turn it off and saw I had a missed call from Ashton. I quickly sent her a text, saying I was sorry I didn't inform her I would be staying at Sabastian's place and would be driving myself to work today. Then not moments later I heard a knocking on the door. Crawling out of bed, I drug my feet the distance to the door. Cracking it open, to avoid letting the harsh hallway light into my room and peaking outside to see a young maid standing outside the door.

She was average height and petite, with light brown hair cut into a bob. She had a heart shaped face with big bright eyes, full lips, and an elvian nose that was cover in very faint freckles. She was wearing a cliché black and white maid's uniform. One of the ones with a black collared dress that came to about mid-thigh, a white apron with lace accents, and white knee-high socks with black Mary-Janes.

"Hello, miss, I didn't wake you, did I?" She said in a sweet spritely voice, smiling ear to ear.

"No, I was already awake." I said still kind of drowsy.

"Good, I hope you had a pleasant night's rest. May I enter?"

"Oh, yes of course, sorry about that." I said opening the door the rest of the way and moving aside.

"My name is Eliza, and I will be at your service during your time here. May I ask your name?"

"It's lovely to meet you Eliza, my name is Jezebel, but Jez is fine too."

"Alright Jez," she said with a bit of a giggle. "I will make the bed now, go about your morning like I am not even here, and don't be afraid to ask me for anything. Breakfast will be ready soon. Would you like Jasper to deliver it or would you like to go down to the dining room?"

"I'll go downstairs. Thank you!"

"Not a problem miss." She said sweetly and then walked toward the bed and began remaking it. Then awkwardly I walked past her to the bathroom, not quite sure how to react, so I moved on like she wasn't even there, like she'd instructed.

I washed my face and brushed my teeth, taking my time with both, enjoy my time. I looked at my hair and ran my fingers through it debating whether I was good to not shower. Deciding I'd be good for at least another day, I went back out to the room to see that Eliza had finished and left the room.

I went to the bench to grab my clothes to find they were gone, I looked around the room to be sure they weren't moved. After assuring myself that they were gone, I realized that Eliza must have taken them to be washed. I stood in the same spot for a couple minutes before walking to the wardrobe. Opening the bottom drawers, that I had not yet looked inside of. Exactly as I'd expect there were t-shirts and tank tops in one draw and jeans, shorts in the other. I picked out an outfit, got dressed, brushed my hair and pulling it up into the usually daily messy bun. Took one last look in the mirror and headed out the door for breakfast.

As I was leaving my room, just outside the door, I quite literally ran into Sebastian knocking him to the ground and landing on top of him. Lifting myself with my arms I looked at him, and blushed.

"Good morning!" He said cheerfully with a chuckle, from beneath me.

"Good morning!" I said with a smiling climbing back to my feet, and then helping him up. "Sorry about that, I didn't realize you were there. Don't vampires sleep during the day?"

"That's okay. Yes, they do, and I would be if I could sleep. I haven't really slept well for the past 30 years or so. So that not that long but still quite some time." Sebastian explained.

"Oh, I'm sorry." I stated sincerely.

"Don't be, I have the rest of my immortality to catch up." He joked, then continued, "I just came to tell you breakfast was ready. I wanted to give you a personal escort.

"Well let's go then, I love breakfast it's my favorite." Then I followed him as he made his way down the hall. "I am actually glad you came to get me. I probably would have gotten lost. There are so many hallways I am going to need a map."

"I understand, it took a few years to get to know my way as well." I smiled at him then he changed the subject, "I see you've taken a liking to your wardrobe."

Then after first looking down at my clothing I added, "Um, yes I didn't really have a choice. Eliza had escaped with my clothes before I could say anything. I suppose it's for the best though considering they are for me, right?"

"Yes, she is very thorough. They are for you; I hope they are alright."

"I mean there are some things that aren't quite my style," I said mostly joking.

"Feel free to leave them out and I will have them returned. If you'd like you can go over what you would prefer with Eliza, and she will get replacements while she is there."

"I was mostly kidding, but that actually sounds okay."

Then we walked into the dining room to see the table that was already set for breakfast. Walking behind Sebastian to my seat, who had pulled out my chair for me. I sat at the table to see a glass of orange juice, a plate of wheat toast with a bowl of butter and jam portions (like in a restaurant), a small bowl filled with fruit to the side. A bigger bowl full of cream of wheat in the center, with a teaspoon of brown sugar sitting in the center ready to be mixed.

"This looks lovely." I said gratefully.

"I am glad it pleases you; I wasn't sure what you like. So, I had to guess, I seem to be particularly good at it."

"I agree." I said before taking a sip of my juice and then starting to eat my fruit bowl.

"What kinds of things do you like to eat normally?"

"For breakfast?" I inquired, not quite sure what he was asking.

"For all meals."

"Oh um, I follow a pretty basic paleo diet," then in a whisper I stated, "but sometimes I cheat because I love sweets." I said with a guilty, yet proud grin, making him laugh out loud.

Then as I had finished, and Jasper had cleared away the empty dishes. I stared at Sebastian who looking over and signing some paperwork, with another male servant. After he finished signing, the servant gathers the bundle of papers and carried them away. I followed him with my eyes until he left through the door. Then looking back to Sebastian, I stated, "Are you not going to eat anything?"

"No, thank you." He said plainly.

"You don't have to be embarrassed you know, I don't mind." Blushing slightly, he began looking away with wandering eyes, trying to contain his shame. "I mean it, I honestly don't mind."

Then he signaled to Jasper, who was standing just outside the kitchen doors, with a nod. Jasper disappeared into the kitchen and returned with a large raw steak. He places the plate down in front of Sebastian.

Sebastian grabbed the steak with his hands and lifted it above his face. Then clamped on to it sinking his sharp fangs into the bottom. I waited patiently for him to finish, trying hard not to stare. Instead, I studied the small center piece of roses. They were cut with 4-inch stems and placed in the sphere-shaped crystal vase in front of us. It was hard to focus seeing as all I could hear is him slurping on the steak. Then I heard a thud sound as he dropped the dehydrated meat back onto the plate.

"Feel better?" I asked, as he wipe his mouth and hands with a towel.

"Yes, thank you." He spoke timidly, still avoiding eye contact.

"Can I ask you something?"

"Of course." He said looking back up at me once again grateful of my ability to change the subject.

"If you can't eat food? Then why did you on the night you'd had me over for a date?"

"I hadn't don't you remember I didn't touch my food, I only made it seem like I had. But secretly Jasper had filled my glass with fresh blood, instead of wine." Then thinking back to the night, I realized he was right, he didn't ever actually put the food in his mouth.

"If you can drink it from a glass, then why the steak?" I asked profusely curious.

Then he cleared his throat, clearly uncomfortable with the conversation but continuing to answer me anyway. "I like the taste better; the fatty tissue of the steak adds flavor and keeps it fresh."

"Oh, that make sense." Then Sebastian grinned and ran his fingers through his long hair, charmed by my honest carefree attitude toward his special dietary needs.

Then the grandfather clock just behind me went off, it was seven o'clock. "I should probably head to work if I want to get through traffic and make it on time. I can't be late for my second day, can I?"

"Thank you, Sebastian, for everything, I will be back for lessons tonight." I said before getting up from the dining table and headed toward the door. Then before leaving I turned and said, "Oh I will let you know the details of the double date. Knowing Ashton, she'll spring it on us last minute."

"Okay, I will be ready for whatever."

"Bye." Then I left the room with Eliza in toe, and she discussed with me the wardrobe changes. Then I collected my things from my room and headed back to the front of the mansion and out the front door. I made it to the theatre fifteen minutes before rehearsal were scheduled to start. Ready for yet another amazing day in my new job, if only I knew what I was in for.

CHAPTER

XXVI

I walk into the performance hall to see Ashton playing with the props on stage cuddling a paper cup of coffee, and the janitor vacuuming the aisles. I climbed up the stairs to the stage and approaching silently.

"Hello, and good morning." I said from behind her, making her jump and almost spill her coffee with my sudden presence. "Sorry, I seem to be doing that a lot today."

"Not its fine, so I got your message that you stayed at Sebastian's last night."

"Yes, he is helping with my magic, as you know, and he didn't want me driving home in the dark exhausted. Which he was right, it drains a lot out of you, especially at first."

"Oh, so did anything happen?" she said with a suggestive tone.

"No! Nothing like that, and I stayed in my own room actually. Which is gorgeous by the way!"

"He gave you your own room! Where does he live?"

"He lives in the huge house that is a few miles out of town."

"Wow, well done Jez, well done." She said clearly impressed, then looking me up and down she noticed my new clothes. "Cute outfit!" She teased with a sarcastic tone.

"Thank you!" I sassed her back knowing exactly what she meant. "I needed something to wear, and I think he has good taste. So, what are you doing here so early?" I asked looking at the empty theatre.

"Oh, I thought I had some last-minute scheduling and orders to make but turns out I had already done it. So now I'm kind of wasting time. I even had time to walk down to the Starbucks a couple blocks down and make it back before we started."

"Wow, how efficient of you. Oh, by the way, Sebastian agreed to double with us, so whenever you're ready let me know. Just remember he has a sever sensitivity to sunlight."

Then really excited and relieved, almost choking on her hot coffee, she exclaimed. "That's great! And of course, no one does morning dates anyway. How does tonight sound?" Then standing wide eyed waiting for my response.

"Called it!" I gloated under my breath as if Sebastian were in the room.

"What?" she said confused.

"Nothing, um tonight sound great! I will tell Sebastian to cancel lessons. Did you want us to all go together or did you want to go separate..."?

"Together!" she shouted cutting me off.

"Okay? Why do you want to go out with this guy if you can't even be alone with him?"

Then she signed and said, "It's Damien."

"You mean the guy you were seeing when we first met. The guy who used you and that, thanks to me, you were finally able to see he was a no-good loser and rise a stronger independent woman. That Damien?"

"Yes." She squeaked.

"Why!" I blurted, "Why would you do this to yourself? You know what he did to you?"

"Yes, I know, but I swear he is different this time."

"That is was you said every time! I don't think it is physically possible for a person to change that much, that often. Do you?"

"I swear this time is different!" she said defensively, completely avoiding the question.

"Then why can you not go on a date by yourself with him?"

"Okay, your right okay! I wanted to go on a test date with him but not make it obvious that it is in fact a date-date. I want to see if he is worth another shot."

"I can have told you that. No!" Then we stood silently for a while, and the other actors started to walk onto the stage. I looked at her as she pouted, and my firm heart softened just enough to give in. Then I grumbled, "okay, fine I will go, but just know I am only doing this because I love you!"

"Yes! Thank you, Jezebel!" Said excitedly and then wrapping me in a tight hug. Then one of the other cast members interrupted us with a question she had about her role. So, in agreeance with our eyes we parted ways. As she began to walk away with the other cast member Linda approached me.

"Yer costume is finished, and ready to be tried on." The she gestured for me to follow her, I did accordingly. As we made the trip to the dressing room, she made small talk with me. "How was yer nicht love?"

"Oh, it was good." I said surprised by the question, not sure else what to say.

"Guid. Dae ye have yerself a boyfriend?"

Then realizing that I didn't really know her I felt comfortable enough to admit my true feelings. Knowing she wouldn't know otherwise, "Yes, I would call him that."

"I bit he's a looker, he is." She teased in her regular chipper way.

"Oh, yes!" I exclaimed, knowing it wasn't a question, but feeling inclined to answer anyway. She just made a squealing noise, surprised by my response, and then laughed.

Then we made it to the room and I went to a changing stall and put on my costume. It fit even more perfect than it had before. I looked at myself in the mirror, twirling as I saw the beautiful sparkling costume on myself. Feeling so ecstatic to bring this character to life. Then stepping out of the changing stall I walked into the main part of the room. I noticed Linda talking with another cast member. I waited patiently for them to finish talking. I began looking around the room daydreaming, then I heard someone say something to me.

"Hello, you must be our new fairy." I turned to look at him, he was smiling at me as Linda ran back to the closet area.

"Yes, I am the black fairy. What part do you play?"

"I am a troll, and a knight."

"Oh, you have two parts."

"Yes, the troll dies in the beginning so then I became one of the knights." I nodded impressed by the fact that he had two parts, and he interrupted my train of thought again.

"So do you have a name, or should I just call you Fairy?"

I giggled at his icebreaker, "Sorry, I seem to be a space case today. My name is Jezebel."

"It's nice to meet you, I'm Callan." He said as he stuck out his hand for me to shake it, I shook it as he looked my costume over.

Then letting go I said, "Is there something wrong with it?"

"No, it's perfect." He said before winking at me and then cocking a sideways grin and looking me up and down once more. Then before I was about to slap him for being a perv, Linda came to my rescue.

Thumping him in the chest with the back of her hand, and remarked "Ye stop that now, this one's taken."

"Oh, she's taken is she?"

"Aye, so ye best do ye pickin' elsewhaur." Then giving me the lady look. You know the one where she tells you she's got your back with her eyes and brows, while perking her lips out and nodding slightly.

"She speaks the truth." I said struggling my shoulders feeling grateful knowing there was more estrogen in the room, than testosterone.

"That's too bad. So how about we be friends then?"

"I am not gonna turn down friendship." Then I blushed and smiled at him, as someone knocked on the door, it was Ashton.

"Come on in, join the party boss." Callan said as if he had ownership of the room suddenly.

She entered, looking at Linda, then looking at me. "Oh, that looks great!"

"Aye, I had to make the shoulders smaller. I even brought in the waistline a bit to tailor to her breast and add support. Would nae want her to lose a bosom while hangin' from the harness, now, would we?" she said with a laugh.

Then feeling incredibly awkward as Linda had talked about my boobs flying out in front of Callan. Who was now undressing me with his eyes as she spoke? Ashton, noticing my awkwardness and its cause, she turned to Callan and said. "Is there something you needed?"

Then as he was about to say something Linda chimed in once more, "Aye, that's mah faut loove." Then Linda handed Callan a pair of lime green tights. "Haur ye go and try nae to rip them again." He took them and then made his grand exit by winking one last time at me. Then he disappeared heading down the hall toward the stage.

Then Ashton and I both looked at each other unsure of how to react, so we ignored the matter altogether. "So, are you ready to get this practice going?"

"Yup, let's do this." I said overdramatically with a nod, then we both said our goodbyes to Linda and made out way to the stage.

Practice went well, and I was finally starting to get the hang of it when someone yelled, "Watch out!" Pushing me out of the way knocking me to the ground. I fell so hard my hand made a screeching sound as they slide across the stage. Then I rolled over to see a huge, weighted burlap bag, that is used in the pully system of the curtains and props. It was sitting on the stage exactly where I had been standing.

I join the rest of the cast who was already looking up to see what caused it to fall. But the top of the stage was so high and dark it was hard to see anything. Then I noticed something strange as I looked at the beams that went over the stage, something familiar that gave me chills of trauma. Being one of the two people here who had ever seen something like that I just brushed it off to not call attention to it and put anyone in danger. Then Callan, walked over to me and helped me to my feet, and asked if I was alright. I nodded, unsure if I was alright finding it hard to shake away what I saw but nodded anyway. Then after no one could figure how it had happened, and we were sure I was alright everyone moved on with rehearsal.

The show must go on as they say, so practices continued without any disturbances, but I kept the image of what I saw in the back of my mind and never let my guard down. During one of my off scenes, I was practicing the steps to my ritual spell for the play. Mostly to be sure I didn't use any actual magic and burn the place down. I moved about the back-stage area when I heard a strange noise. I paused to investigate and recognized the sound of squeaky wheels. I turned to my left to see the coffee cart, that is keep backstage, speeding toward me at an accelerated rate. Thankfully, I was able to move out of the way in time for it not to run me over. Unfortunately, that meant it continuing past me into the wall, not only making a loud clanging noise, but a huge mess.

I look around to see people suddenly gathering around me to see what is going on yet again. Ashton rushing into the scene to assess the situation and remark. "Well, you're just a magnet for negative energy today, aren't you?" I say nothing just remaining focused on what I saw earlier in the rafters wandering if this was related. Ashton clearly seeing my bothered state, makes a last-minute decision and announces we will have an early out today. Then tells everyone to be here bright an early tomorrow. Everyone in the cast and crew scatters, overjoyed by the news.

"Are you okay sweetie?" she asks me gently.

"Yeah, just a little preoccupied. You didn't have to do that on my account."

"Eh, we could use break we practice so hard. Besides, you and I have a date to get ready for. Come on lets go home."

"Okay I'm just gonna grab my bag from my dressing room and change."

"Okay I got'ta close up anyway."

Then heading down the hall, I take out my phone and text Sebastian while I walked. *Hey so I was right Ash sprung it on u. It is tonight. Is that good for you?*

I got a response back within a few moments, *Yes of course! Where and when? -SB*

We are going to all meet up at 6-ish at our loft and walk to this great place a few blocks away.

Sounds wonderful. Also, would it be alright if I show up a little early, I have something I would like to give you. -SB

Then jokingly I teased, *You know you can stop giving me things now, right?*

It's not that kind of something -SB

Okay, yeah its fine. I responded a little nervous of what it could be.

I put my phone back in my pocket and turned into my dressing room, changed out of my costume and into my regular clothes, that Linda had moved from the costume room. Then I grabbed my bag and started heading out the door. When someone covers my mouth and pulls back into the room. Turing off the lights in the room and closing the door. It is dark and the only like in the room is the dim lights of the vanity.

I struggle to get free, but their grip is too tight I try to scream but they are still covering my mouth. As I struggle, I can feel the persons face next to my ear, they are breathing hard. Then I feel their finger running along my left cheekbone, and all I can see is one long painted fingernail. With one quick motion they break my skin with their fingernail causing me to bleed. That is when I notice it is man by the groan of pleasure he makes as he licks his finger clean of my blood.

I take a deep breath and then instinctively somehow, I know what to do. I take my free arm and jerk it backwards into the man's gut. Then as then began to scrunch from the pain, I grab their hands and in one quick motion lift and spin. So that I now face this infamous strange. Then taking my foot I kick them in the gut where I had just created a weak spot.

They go flying backward into a rack of costumes and boxes that come crashing down on them. Then swiftly toward the crack of light that peaks out from under the closed door. I open it, grabbing bag from the ground next to the doorway, then escaping, running as fast as I can and not looking back. Then I reach the exit of the theater to find Ashton sitting in the car out front waiting for me. I compose myself as I make my way through the lobby.

Then I exit the build trying hard to act like nothing had happened, so that I don't alarm her. I get in the car, and she speeds away from the curb, still not having said any words to each other. I look out the window into the rearview to be sure there is no one behind us. Then I breathe deeply and close my eyes, trying hard not to let the fear get to me that I had been blocking before. Then against my will a single tear rolled down my right cheek.

CHAPTER

XXVII

Ashton and I drove for a couple blocks before she noticed I am being quiet, and something is obviously on my mind. I see her looking at me in glances with my peripherals but ignore her in hopes that she will leave me alone. Then I notice that she has a disturbed look on her face, so I turn to look at her.

"What?" I ask confused, trying to hide my true feeling from more than just her. Then she take her hand and wipe my left cheek and bring it to her face.

"Is this blood?" Then realizing I've been found out; I know I have no choice but to explain. But somehow, I don't know what to say, or even where to begin so ignoring her question I look away. "Jezebel!" she yells at me upset, pulling on my shoulder to bring me back to the conversation.

I turn to her with tears in my eyes feeling overwhelmed with fear, but still having nothing to say. Clearly worried she pulls over to the side of the street. With the car still running, repositions herself in the driver's seat so that she is facing me and says one thing.

"I will not make you tell me anything, ever. I only ask that you understand I support you and ever version of you! This new life you suddenly have is amazing and I remember you telling me how you always hoped for something this, and how crazy that its actually real. I am still having a hard time wrapping my head around it. But don't you think that I am not a part of it. If you honestly feel that you can't tell something, for any reason, I will have to be okay with that. Just know that I worry when you look at me with obvious pain and fear in your eyes, and with blood on your face and say nothing. I will do my best to help you, even if I can't compare to the things you have to face in this new world of yours. I will fight my hardest for you always!" Still, I say nothing, it was as if that part of my brain had completely checked out. My eyes are then overtaken by more tears that stream down my face, feeling every word she said deep in my chest. Eventually I was able to crack a weak smile, and nod to let her know I understand and am listening.

"Alright, as long as you're gonna be better soon, I will trust you. Now let's go home." Then Ashton turn back in her seat and continues driving us home. The car is silent the entire way there yet somehow it felt so loud. Like every thought and emotion was heard by the other without ever having to be spoken aloud.

We finally make it home and up to the loft, as we are walking through the front door, I hear a familiar voice behind me. Looking behind me to see Sebastian's dreamy existence lingering a few feet from where I was standing. I look to Ashton who had also turned to see whose voice it was. I motion to her that it's okay for her to go inside without me and get ready. She nods in agreeance but not before taking one last glance at Sebastian. Giving him a glare, as if sending a warning by some kind of mental signal, then continuing inside.

Standing alone with him in the hall I smiled at him, suddenly feeling better by his presents alone. Completely forgetting the feeling that had complete consumed me and my mind just less than an hour ago at the theatre. Then unexpectedly finding my voice again, I declare, "You are a little early."

"I said I would be." He explains confused by my statement.

"I know, but I didn't think it would be this early." I said as checking the time on my phone to read 4:41pm.

"I know, I am sorry, but as soon as I knew that the sun had set, I couldn't wait to see you, so I came as fast as I could."

"The sun barely set like for 45 minutes ago and it's at least an hour drive from your place. That is assuming traffic is good and I highly doubt it considering the time."

"Who said I drove?" He said grinning at me making the statement seem more dramatic than necessary. Quite successfully however seeing as he had completely stumped me, in turn rendering me speechless.

"Touché," then letting out a slight giggle and turning around and heading inside and turning around expecting to see Sebastian following me, but instead finding him still lingering in the hallway. "Aren't you going to come in?"

"Yes, but I can't..." he said awkwardly.

"Oh, why not, do you not want to go anymore?"

"No, it's not that," he said before laughing, "You have to invite me in."

"Oh, duh, sorry I complete forgot about that rule, why is it exactly that I have to do that?"

"I am not welcome on your private property without an invitation." He gently explained, obviously trying hard to hide his embarrassment but ultimately failing once again.

"Oh, well then you may come in," I stated stepping aside so that he may enter.

Then he started to look around, as I took off my coat and shoes and putting them to the side. Our loft wasn't quite as large as where he lived but it was as nice, maybe not as nice, but still nice. When you step through the front door onto the entryway landing immediately to the right is a long narrow table. The table has a rectangular basket for mail, and a small glass bowl for keys, spare change, and above the table is a large mirror. Then as you enter further you notice the mud bench behind the door for coat, shoes, and bags.

"I know it's not what your used to but believe it or not it used to look a lot worse."

"What do you mean? When Ash and I first became roommates, we lived in this awful one bed apartment downtown. I was more than a fixer upper." I said with a smile.

"If it was only one bedroom then why did you become roommates?"

"It was a studio which took up a whole floor, so the landlord charged a ridiculous amount. Ash couldn't do it on her own and neither of us had a good enough paying job to afford a place of our own. It worked out though living in such tight quarters really helped us to get to know one another. I will say however on some occasions it was more, intimate, than I would have liked. Nevertheless, that experience helped me grow not only with her but as my own person."

"Wow! You two must be really close."

"Inseparable!" I said gleefully with a huge smile.

"Yeah, I can't get rid of her." Ashton chimed in as she entered the room in a bath towel wrapped around her body and another twisted in her hair atop her head.

"You love me." I stated pleasantly as she wrapped her arm around me.

"Yes, I do." Then she turned to Sebastian wasting no time at all to put on her older sister pants and change the subject. "So, I here you're a bloodsucker?"

"Ashton!" I barked, trying to get her to back down and stop being rude.

"Ahem, Yes?" Sebastian responded clearly caught off guard.

"Listen, you," she said on her toes and in his face, waving her finger around like she was scolding him, "I love Jezebel! She is my little sister you hear me, so if you hurt her, I don't care what you are! I will hunt down and I will skin you alive! You got me!"

"Yes ma'am." He responded clearly unphased by her threat, but with complete understanding and respect.

"Good! I'm going to get dressed now! I'm catching a draft!" She said as she exited the room but still not breaking eye contact with Sebastian until she left the room.

"Well, that was dramatic, but nothing ever isn't when Ash is in the room. Anyway, you want a tour?"

"Yes, I would like a tour." He stated as we moved on from the drama.

"Okay as you can see this is the living room." I said in my best tour guide impersonation, as we stepped down from the landing, that stretches along the north wall, same wall as the doorway. He looked over the entire room, decorated with very neutral colors of beige, gray and black, with a hint of personalized colors throughout. There is a gray suede couch at the foot of the landing, a glass coffee table and a flat screen along the south wall, opposite the door. Above the TV is a collection of different mirrors, and then heading to the left of the loft I continued my tour.

"This is the kitchen, we don't really use it all that often, I do however like to bake but don't ever seem to have the time anymore."

"That is too bad, I sure you are a good baker."

"As a matter fact, I am." I retorted in a sassy tone, walking around the center counter of the kitchen waiting for him to review this room as well. The kitchen, like the living room, didn't have much color it was mostly black but in different shades. It is connected to the living room separated by only one partial wall coming from off the north wall. At the entrance of the kitchen was a round four chair table, with a wall of windows to the south, overlooking the city. In the center is a black counter island with three barstools on the same side as the table. Then on the other side of the counter against the north wall, from left to right was the sink, stove/oven, and refrigerator. It also has a few cabinets above the sink and stove.

Then we moved on to the left of the loft around the corner from where the fridge sits against the north wall our tour continues. "This is the bathroom, nothing too exciting about that." Then turning and point to the east end of the loft was another door. "That is Ashton's room, she got the master, takes up this entire end of the apartment."

"Wow, how did she get so lucky?" he teased.

"Oh, I definitely got the better deal." I commented then continuing in my tour guide voice, "If you'll follow me this way, we gonna back track a little." Then cutting back across the kitchen and the living room to the other side of the loft. Toward one of the two doorways that were tucked into the west wall, both doors facing to the south. Entering the one closest to the north wall first. "This is my studio; I say studio not office because it sounds more fun."

Stepping inside the little room he looked around to see my desk in the center and a few bookshelves, and a small couch. Then after I was sure he saw everything, we moved on to the other door. Standing in front of the closed door I turn and look at him blushing a bit. "This is my room."

His eyes brighten as I speak the words, suddenly full of delight. Then I open the door and we enter. Beside the doorway to the left is one of my two nightstands, the other being on the other side of the queen-sized bed, all against the south wall. Then across from my bed is my dresser, along the west wall is my closet. Then finally in the east corner was an armchair. Sitting in front of east wall that was covered with shelfing. The shelves are filled with movie, books, photo albums, journals and some picture frames and knick-knacks.

After he is done looking around the room, he turns to find me sitting crisscross on my bed. Joining me by sitting just in front of me he says, "This is much better than anything I could have ever given you."

"I don't know about that." I say bashfully, "I really love my room at your place, and I love that you wanted me to have it even more."

"You are welcome anytime." He said in a gentle voice, his eyes dazzling me as usual, drawing me in like an insect I lean in a bit. I feel him lean in as well, close enough that I could already anticipate the kiss I knew was about to happen. As if his lips were already locked with mine.

Already closing my eyes and puckering my lips my heart began to race and I prepared myself for the kiss. When suddenly I felt Sebastian move off the bed. Falling into a face full of nothing, I catch myself on the bed where he was sitting. Then opening my eyes to find him sitting in the armchair.

"What's the matter?" I inquired, disappointed I didn't get the kiss.

"I am sorry, I want to kiss you more than anything, but I want to deserve it first. It is crucial that I stay focused and not be distracted by the temptation you arouse in me."

"Who's to say that you don't deserve it."

"Just look at your face! I am the reason that happened to you!" He roared raising to his feet, shocked I touch the scratch on my cheek from the attack earlier. I traced my finger over it feeling the scab form, having completely forgotten it was there.

"How do you know about that?" I said worried about what the answer might be.

"I have you followed sometimes. At the theatre today after you left with obvious blood on your cheek. My inspector stuck around a bit longer to see the person who did that to you leave."

"Do you know who it was?"

"No, but I have a hunch. I'm just hoping I am wrong. I want to be able to protect you but it's really hard when I can only be with you half the time. That leaves you vulnerable the other half."

"I am not a helpless animal; he was lucky to have even got this. Beside I am learning to control my magic. Soon I be able to do even worse than what I did."

"But you shouldn't have to," then rushing to the bed grabbing my hand, "That is my job, and I can't even do it." Then dropped his head in disappointment and anger.

"Your here now." I cried trying my best to console him.

"I can't lose you again, I have waited so long to get you back and now someone is trying to take you from me." He sobbed angrily with his head still hanging down.

"I am not going anywhere you understand me. After everything that has already happen, I should be running for the hills from you, but I'm not. I am sitting right here tell you that I am here to stay." Then perky up he looked me and nodded and simply said.

"You should start getting ready or were gonna be late." Then got up and left the room, pausing in the door, then continuing into the living room.

Feeling frustrated and defeated, I sat on the bed with every intention of storming out of the room and yelling at him, but I knew he was right. So, I closed the door halfway and began pick out something to wear.

CHAPTER

XXVIII

I had been ready for at least fifteen minutes but sat on the end of my bed procrastinating. I could hear Ashton in the living room talking with Damien, her date, and Sebastian. I knew I had to hurry but I felt so unsecure leaving the apartment knowing that the attack earlier was planned. That whoever he was, or they were, is still out there waiting for me to drop my guard. Did I really know what I signed up for when I agreed to except the clan of Sanbellet's power? What did that even mean?

Then thinking about what Sebastian had promised in that small room when he told me who I really was. Then hearing his voice echo in my head as if he were standing in the room, he said.

"I will never hurt you again, you have my word… I am vowing to never bring harm to you or to let another harm you." The voice echoes clear and precise it was exactly what I needed to hear. I have been on my own so long I don't even know what means to have someone that devoted to keeping me safe. Not even when I was with Michael did, I feel that amount of devotion. I grabbed my stomach feeling the flutter of butterflies just thinking about how much Sebastian must care for me.

So finally walking out of my room and into the living room, we all grabbed our things and left the loft. We walked down the street and into the alley to an Arcade Bar. A new up a coming business called Arcadia Alley that was owned by one of Ashton's friends, Samantha. She opened alongside her life partner Beverly. It is the coolest place for an adult to exist, and least that what it says on the sign. Personally, I never really cared for arcade games, or games in general for that matter.

However, you get free drinks, food and even prizes depending on the amount of tickets you win. The only catch is you are allowed only a certain number of coins per person, decreasing your chances of winning prizes. I had only ever been there once and didn't really enjoy it because I was preoccupied with some work I had to do, so left early. Not quite sure how I should feel about going back, I don't even know Samantha or Beverly that well. But this is Ashton's wish and after what I had done to her a few days ago I feel like I have a debt to pay. One I may be paying for the rest of my existence.

We enter the bar, being hit suddenly with black lights, the sounds of arcades games and 80's music. After paying the cover charge, getting our hands stamped and receiving a roll of coins (included in your cover charge) we make our way through the crowd of people toward the bar.

"Hey, long time no see!" Samantha shouts from behind the bar to Ashton, who then takes a seat inviting Damien to sit beside her. Feeling suddenly like a third wheel not really knowing what to do with myself or even where I am welcome.

"Do you want to play a game?" Sebastian shouts over the music.

"I don't really play games." I stated still feeling uneasy.

"Oh, come on, it'll be fun.

"Okay, fine." I say caving into his luring voice and smile. I wave to Ashton who seems to be hitting off with Damien and reconnecting with Samantha.

Sebastian and I walked around to find an open game to play and feeling like we hit the lottery when there was an open ski ball. Putting in a couple coins, he started to play quickly racking up points, not missing a single hole.

"How are you so good at this?" I said amazed at his hidden talent.

"Come on really? I have had *years* of practice." He retorted in a cocky voice bragging about his abilities. I started laughing at him uncontrollably not holding anything back, suddenly feeling comfortable in my environment. "What is so funny?" he said amused by my snickering.

"You just became even more of a dork." I giggled, having to grab my stomachs aching muscles.

"You're gonna pay for that!" He said tickling my already aching sides, making me laugh even harder until I snorted. Surprising both of us, making us look at each other with blank expressions for a moment, before both braking out in laughter. Then as the laughter calmed to just bright smiles, he resumed his game.

"Teach me?" I chimed in, after watching him for a couple of minutes.

"Do you not know how to play?"

"No, sorry."

"I am excellent teacher, as you know. Come here?" he said opening his arm to me.

Approaching him, he placed his hands on my sides positioning me in front of him and placing the ball in my right hand. Then showing me the motion of what to do with my arm before letting go of the ball. Then backing away to let me give it a try, I fling the ball and make it in the 1000 hole on my first try. Then jumping up and down, like a cheerleader, celebrating my victory.

"I sense foul play." He said teasing me while smirking.

"Are you suggesting I used my ma…" then realizing my words I quietly rerouted them, "my talents?"

"Yes, that is exactly what I think." He stated in a mocking tone.

"Sorry to disappoint but it seems I have more than just a few talents to offer." Then grabbing the tickets and heading back toward the bar. Taunting him with them as if he were a dog and they were his treat.

We dodged and weaved through the other people playing games or just standing around. I reached my hand back to him, so that he might grab it, so we don't get separated in the bar. Feeling his cold hand grab mine we continued to the bar. The bar was finally insight when Sebastian stopped abruptly. I turned to find out what the holdup was.

"What is the matter?" I asked, seeing him obviously scanning the crowd for something specific.

"I thought I saw, never mind. Come on." Then pushing past me still holding my hand rushing toward the bar and out of the crowd.

We made to the bar, and I offered up my tickets to Ash who was elbows deep in her French fries.

"Look at you are scoring point, and winning tickets," she said with a wink.

"Actually, most of them are Sebastian's." I said looking over my shoulder to see him standing behind me. Then back to Ash who was already trading them for free drinks.

"Would you like anything hun?" Samantha asked me.

"Umm, yeah I'll take an order of fries and an iced tea, thank you!" Then she looked at Sebastian, "How about you hun?"

"No, thank you." Then tearing off the tickets, she went back to prepare orders.

Then I looked back at Sebastian to see him looking around in the crowd again.

"Sebastian?" I barked. "What are you looking for?"

"Nothing." He said plastering on a fake smiling, I let him get away with it only not to make a scene and ruin the night. Then Samantha walked over placing the basket of fresh fries and cold tea in front of me, and I started digging in.

"Sam was telling me about their new mirror maze, they had installed a few months back." Ashton beamed to me excitedly.

"Wow! I remember when I was little, we went to a mirror, and I loved it!" I cheered thrillingly, before stuffing my face with more fries.

"Hey, I got'ta pee, will you come with me?" Ashton begged.

"Yeah!" Then looking to Sebastian to be sure I could leave him with Damien. Getting and affirmative nod, Ashton and I head to the bathroom.

Making our way to the bathroom, which is not only infinitely colder that the rest of the bar but also quieter. It still had the same black lighting as the rest of the bar however, which made going to the bathroom quite awkward. After we finished, we made our way back to the bar, only a few feet from out seats I notice Sebastian is gone. I look around for him as Ashton climbs back onto her chair.

"Did you see where Sebastian went?" I asked Damien, who shook his and then rejoined the conversation with Samantha and Ashton. Then I receive an anonymous text. *'Come to the maze alone or he gets hurt!'* I look around for any sign of who could have sent it.

Then I rush off to without saying a word, and I rack my brain for a plan. But mostly I send out a silent prayer to whoever could be listening. Hoping that I get to him in time. He vowed to protect me well it was my turn to protect him.

Chapter

XXIX

S till standing in the middle of the bar scanning the room for who could have sent me that text. Not moments later I receive another, *'Time is running out!'* Then I hastily make my way toward the maze, my heart racing at the idea of some hurting him. My gut yelling me the entire time, saying that it was right for not wanting to come out tonight. Being selfish only thinking about what could have happened to me. Not realize I am equally responsible for not letting anything happen to Sebastian.

I make it to the entrance of the maze, and I pause feeling my phone vibrate in my hand, *'Tick-tock princess'* is all it says. So, without hesitation I look behind me to be sure I am not being followed, I enter the maze. Making my way down a long hallway I suddenly come to a fork in the pathway. Not sure whether I should go left or right I close my eyes and trying to decide. When unexpectedly a blue splash of light appears from my right hand.

Flying in front of me toward the left pathway. I follow the small ball of light, not quite sure what it is or where it came from, but somehow knowing that it means no harm.

Turning corners and running my hand along the mirror to be sure I know the direction of the maze. Following the blue light as my guide, delving deeper and deeper into the maze. Seeing nothing but the black lights, the blue light in front of me and my own reflection. Turning a corner when suddenly the light evaporates, and I suddenly stop and look around to be sure I didn't miss it turn. Then having lost my footing and not knowing which way I was going I begin to panic.

Closing my eyes again like I did before hoping for the light to reappear, feeling no surge of magical energy. I am overcome by hopelessness but determined to get Sebastian back I try once more. Standing with my eyes closed when someone comes at me in the dark, startling me by wrapping their arms around me, making me scream. Then they placed their hand over my mouth to quiet me, I looked at this person in the dark. It was Sebastian, my eyes suddenly brighten with relief.

"What are you doing?" I shout at him, as I look him over seeing that he is bleeding on his face and arms. "Oh my god! Sebastian!"

"Jezebel, I need you to be quiet." He whispers bluntly.

"Why? What is going…" then begin cut off his hand coving my mouth once more, his amber eye not leaving mine. I could tell he was listening for something, then coming down from my high, I listen with him. Looking around him, to see only myself in the mirror. Then suddenly hearing a familiar chuckle, I gasp from under Sabbatians cold hand pressed to my face.

"Shhh, quiet." He says in a whisper before lowering his hand. Then turning around and boxing me in against the mirror with his body and arms.

We stand in silence for a moment, suddenly something grabs my leg and pulls me away. I see Sebastian notice my absence shortly after I am gone. As I am being dragged away with yet again someone's hand over my mouth. He is twisting and turning in panic, not sure where to go. Instinctively I make a fireball with my hand to signal my location.

"Stupid witch!" I hear my kidnapper yell at me, before stomping on my hand forcing the flame out and making me shriek in pain. Not soon enough however, seeing Sebastian catching up to us. Then him leaping over me to my captor, tackling him to the ground crashing into the mirrors and shattering the glass.

Still not having seen a face I lay on the ground wincing at the pain at my hand, saying over and over again to myself. "Thearapevo, thearapevo, thearapevo." Feeling my pain suddenly vanish as if it was never really there. Then I feel Sebastian grab me from the ground and lift me to my feet as we ran, trying to find our way out.

"What is going on?" I shout in confusion to Sebastian.

"I think this daydream has just became a nightmare!" He shouts back to me as speeding through the maze. Finding it surprisingly easier for someone who doesn't have a reflection. Then I looked behind us to see if someone was there. Seeing no one made me more scared that if I had, which only made the situation worse.

Thinking to myself that he was right, I thought I knew what I was getting myself into, but I didn't have the slightest idea. I went from being a normal person to a powerful witch overnight. My life was about to take a wild ride in a much different world surrounded by the world I thought I knew.

Then feeling completely torn between who I want to be and who I should be, feeling ripped of my identity once more. Confused and overcome with defeat I didn't understand how I could possibly get everything I ever wanted. Only to feel the same negative way again not days, or even moments later in an entirely different world. Then turning to stare at my reflection in the mirror not even recognizing the person I saw.

Finally finding the way out, we pushed and shoved our way through the mindless horde of people. I looked over to the bar to see Ashton laughing with Damien and feeling a tear rolling down my cheek as I ran for my life. Feeling for the first time that she might not get to be a part of it. Then being overwhelm not only with fear of death, but fear of heartbreak looking at the one person I had always had. Looking away feeling my heart already start to crack thinking about it. See her laugh and smile not even aware of me or my situation. She could live without me, I could make it so, but couldn't I live without her.

Looking to Sebastian who was still gripping my hand tightly. I refocused on the matter at hand, wiping my face clean and gritting my teeth. We made it out the main door down the alley, running straight to the fire escape. Sebastian leaping for the ladder and then climbing up.

"What are we doing?" I stammered confused.

"Just trust me!" He shouted, as we weaved our way back and forth up the metal stairs, to the roof. Then as we made it to the roof, a guy crashed to the ground in front of us from the sky. Sebastian shielding me with his body from the stranger, but still peeking around him to get a good look at him.

The guy is tall, with blood red colored hair that is flowing in the breeze of the night, and intense yellow eyes, like a snake. Wearing only a brown leather trench coat with a big hood and tight black skinny jeans with combat boots. His chest completely exposed to the night, with a wide scar a crossed his chest. He stood glaring at us like a hungry beast, licking his chops. I could see his tongue toying with the sharp fangs that hung from his mouth. Looking him up and down my attention caught by his nails. They are long, sharp, and painted with pitch-black nail polish. Clinging to Sebastian, who was still bleeding, feeling afraid not only for me but for him.

He stood his ground however staring at this guy, who stood to challenge him I could feel Sebastian's body start to tremble.

They locked eyes neither one moving and muscle, not even so much as a blink from either guy. There was tension between them, like somehow, they knew each other. Seeing from the fangs that hung from this stranger's month I was not surprised. Having final confirmation that I was right when I looked up to the rafters of the theater to see a pair of blood red eyes, and thinking I'd seen another vamp.

Snarling at each other they both suddenly becoming the fierce predators they are, both there fangs showing and there eye beam the blood red color of danger. They stood like statues in the moonlight, not uttering a single word until Sebastian finally opened his mouth and growled a single word. Make this stranger grin with pleasure at the sound of it.

"Thaddeus!"

THE END…for now